D0940335

THE PULL OF THE MOON

the Moon

stories

Julie Paul

BRINDLE
&GLASS

Copyright © 2014 Julie Paul

All rights reserved. No part of this publication may be reproduced, stored in
a retrieval system, or transmitted in any form or by any means—electronic,
mechanical, recording, or otherwise—without the prior written consent
of the publisher or a licence from the Canadian Copyright Licensing Agency
(ACCESS Copyright). For a copyright licence, visit accesscopyright.ca.

Brindle & Glass Publishing Ltd.
brindleandglass.com

LIBRARY AND ARCHIVES CANADA CATALOGUING IN PUBLICATION
Paul, Julie, 1969–, author
The pull of the moon : stories / Julie Paul.

Issued in print and electronic formats.
ISBN 978-1-927366-32-5

I. Title.

PS8631.A8498P85 2014   C813'.6   C2014-902773-7

Editor: Holley Rubinsky
Proofreader: Heather Sangster, Strong Finish
Design: Pete Kohut
Author photo: Ryan Rock

We gratefully acknowledge the financial support for our publishing activities from
the Government of Canada through the Canada Book Fund and the Canada
Council for the Arts, and from the Province of British Columbia through the
British Columbia Arts Council and the Book Publishing Tax Credit.

The interior pages of this book have been printed on 100% post-consumer
recycled paper, processed chlorine free, and printed with vegetable-based inks.

This book is a work of fiction. Names, characters, places, and incidents are either
products of the author's imagination or are used fictitiously. Any resemblance to
actual events or locales or persons, living or dead, is entirely coincidental.

1 2 3 4 5 18 17 16 15 14

PRINTED IN CANADA

For Ryan and Avery Jane,
~Ziggy Two-Socks.

CONTENTS

✳ ✳ ✳

Black Forest

Jenny didn't want to go to the market. "They have too many weird vegetables there," she told her father, Lawrence. Jenny was a sensitive kid, and many things were weird to her, and Lawrence and Vicki had made numerous concessions, such as taking the toothpaste out of the tube when they brought it home from the store. They squeezed it all out into a jar with a tight-fitting lid, a tiny spoon on the side, and each time they needed toothpaste they scooped it out and spread it on the brush. This was one example of hundreds.

Lawrence needed to shop for food but didn't want to leave Jenny at home alone. She was eleven going on sixteen going on five. No babysitting club for this girl. "If you come, I'll buy you a gelato," he told her. "The best in Montreal."

"It has to be lemon, Daddy," she said.

"I'm sure they have lemon."

"Call ahead," she said.

Lawrence knew the little stand in the middle of Jean-Talon Market had no phone, but he said he would try. He pretended to call from his bedroom while Jenny got dressed. "Merci," he said to the dial tone. "A bientôt."

Jenny came out of her room wearing long johns, a pink net skirt, and a giant sweatshirt announcing, "California!" across her chest. She wore her mini backpack purse, and around her neck hung the blue and pink silk scarf she had cut holes into, to wear as a mask in case she spotted anyone she knew, or if she wanted to be invisible—when the world outside her body was not where she wanted to be. She was old enough to realize that nothing could prevent people from seeing her, especially in her getup. But she told Lawrence she didn't have any other options.

Options. How long since he'd had options? Three months. Three months since the Wii—suddenly too loud, too assaulting, too much for Vicki—had sailed down the back steps into the garden, and then, shortly after, Vicki was sailing down the front steps and into the car—the family's only car—and driving away from them. They had talked on the phone, because phone calls were allowed every so often from the meditation centre somewhere in eastern Ontario where she was gathering herself. Healing in the quietude, according to the catalogue of benefits on the website. Becoming mindful, connected to the entire universe, at peace in every moment.

Every moment? Every single, solitary moment? With Jenny, a moment could last an hour. A moment of peace was higher on his list of needs than a lover's touch. Jenny had become an appendage since Vicki left. She was like a baby, needing to be close to someone at all times, even while she slept. He could understand that, intellectually. But moment to moment, he just needed a bit of space. Just a day, here and there. Even an hour.

Before they left for the market, in the name of exercising his options, Lawrence did his pec stretches in the doorframe. Jenny asked him to dictate his list to her, so there wouldn't be any minutes wasted once they got there. Once upon a time, he and Vicki used to wander through the stalls for hours, executing the style of marketing he preferred: hand in hand, sampling the cut-up apples, the maple taffy, the squeakiest cheese curds, deciding on dinner according to whim and chance.

"Eggs, bread, jam," he said. She wrote down "E, B, and J."

He pushed his mind ahead to the brunch he was planning for

the following day, when Vicki was coming over. She was back in town and wanted to visit. It would be their first attempt to bring themselves into working order, a return to the land of functioning people who live together and don't throw tantrums or plants or video games. Would a roasted vegetable frittata do it?

"Japanese eggplants," he said. Jenny wouldn't eat the big ones—they were too fat.

Dessert would be fruit and ice cream. "Raspberries."

She stuck out her tongue and blew him one. "What else?" she asked, tapping her purple pen on her dog stationery.

"Potatoes," Lawrence said. "And peppers." He could never resist the solid primary colours of the market's bell peppers. A rainbow in a basket.

Lawrence was not optimistic about the meeting. He and Jenny hadn't changed. If Vicki was different, or even if she was the same, how would anything get better? Every time they'd talked on the phone, after they were done chit-chatting about Jenny's latest passions and aversions, he'd asked her: So, when are you coming home? And every time, she'd said she didn't know, until last weekend, when she'd said she would be returning to Montreal in a few days. Where, exactly? A friend's house. Do I know this friend? He did. It was a girlfriend, she said. It was totally fine.

Okay, but what did "fine" mean to her? Did it mean that she didn't want to come back to him, or that she didn't know if she could parent with him any more? Had he even thought about the fact that they had been *parenting* together, before she left? He was Jenny's father, he did what needed to be done; Vicki was the mother of this intensely odd and brainy child, and they'd spent the last eleven years trying to keep from leaping off the Champlain Bridge.

The thing was, he couldn't put his finger on anything he'd done that would make her hate him. Nothing new, anyway. He was the same old Lawrence, just trying to keep everyone happy without going crazy himself. If that included the odd video game played with Jenny or without, was that so wrong? He still spent a lot of time making music on his three guitars when he wasn't working from home for the software company that had generously allowed him to be flexible with hours and location. He still read books. He still knew how to do downward dog.

Could the rift in their relationship ever mend when those traits Vicki had once accepted as being a part of him, so endearingly opposite to hers, were what had made her leave?

He still wanted his family to work.

And did he miss Vicki? His wife, who also drove him mad at times but knew how to kiss his neck in the spot that made him moan? His wife, who laughed when he put underwear on his head and a sock on his penis? His wife, who'd married him all those years ago even though he was small town and she was big city?

He did.

They had been the family who walked their baby to sleep in a sling, around and around the blocks, even in sub-zero temperatures, because that was the only sure way of getting her down. It got to be a joke in their Plateau neighbourhood: Lawrence doing this crazy walk at all hours, dressed like a dogsledder with a hot-pink sling across his chest, a hidden child swaddled inside. Oh, if his hockey buddies back in his small Ontario town could have seen him then!

Then she stopped being an infant and they still did it, or rather, Lawrence did it; Jenny became a heavy baby, then a squirmy toddler, and still, she would only sleep while strapped to a moving body. People talked. His joints ached with the effort. His back would never be the same. But Jenny needed her sleep, and Vicki was convinced that she would cry all night if left in a crib like any other child, and Vicki could not stand to hear her cry.

Not because she thought it was bad for Jenny. Vicki was just so sensitive to noise. He could not call it hypersensitive, at least not to her face, but during the three months without her, Lawrence had finally been able to pee standing up. Would he remember to sit down again tomorrow, when everything was riding on his behaviour, or would his inner rebel keep him standing?

"Asiago cheese," he told Jenny. "And a bottle of white wine."

"I'm not writing that down," she told him. "You're going to corrupt me. Do you want me to end up on the street?"

Lawrence winced and went deeper into the stretch so she would think it was muscle pain.

"When Mom gets here tomorrow," Jenny told Lawrence, "I'm going to do my new routine."

She had sock puppets and she liked to make them act out fairy tales, usually the ones that involved waking up a sleeping princess with a kiss. They were abridged versions, but not by much. Lawrence had to sit on his hands when he watched her shows so he wouldn't make that hurry-up motion, brushing the air toward him.

"I'm sure she'd like that," he said. "But I don't know how much time she'll have." He wanted to prepare her, to make sure she knew that Vicki might not be staying, but he didn't want to freak her out, either. Her mother was coming home.

Jenny nodded. "I'll keep my expectations low."

How can an eleven-year-old know enough to say a thing like this and yet not be able to be alone in a room?

"Plus," Jenny added, "you'll want some time to yourselves." She wiggled her eyebrows.

"Okay," said Lawrence, coming out of his stretch. "Let's jet." He was not in the headspace to talk about sex right then, on top of everything else. Jenny had the books, and Vicki had been good about giving her the facts, years ago, but last week Jenny had asked, over breakfast, how exactly the penis got into the vagina, and if you had to use your hands to stick it in. He added the conversation to his mental list of things to tell Vicki tomorrow, if the mood was right.

Well, timing *and* mood. He knew the equation. Jenny would have to be out of the room.

"Do you have the cloth bags?" Jenny asked once they were outside.

"Oops. Good thinking. Could you get them?"

She bounded back into the apartment, singing "O mio babbino caro." He walked down the stairs to the sidewalk and sat on the bottom step.

Mia from across the street called, "Bonjour!" Lawrence could see, even from his distance, that she was wearing a ruby camisole under her black T-shirt. It peeked out from above the deep V of her neckline.

"Allo," he called back, waving lightly.

"Ça va bien?" she asked.

"Oui, oui. Et vous?"

Jenny slammed the door and scowled at Lawrence. "Hey!" she yelled at Mia. "He's a married man!"

Lawrence sighed. "We were just saying hello."

"Uh-huh. Right."

Had Mia understood? They had only spoken French to each other on recycling days, and once in the winter, when her shovel had broken, he had loaned her his to dig out her car. Now she was still smiling as she watered her planters. Either she didn't understand Jenny or else she just thought she was *fou braque*. Not just crazy—completely nuts. Some days Lawrence wasn't sure. Had they allowed this to happen, he and Vicki, part of the problem instead of the solution? And what was the solution to the problem of a unique child? Was it a problem at all? Where he'd come from, she would have been moulded long before now into a more compliant kid, someone who could tie her shoes herself and handle a paper route, reserving her costumes for Halloween and school plays. But they were worlds away from that kind of life. This was Montreal.

This life, created largely because he'd fallen in love with a smart and sassy girl from here, someone who knew how to navigate cultural duality in her sleep. He'd been smitten by her quirky, off-the-wall intensity; how could he have expected their child to be any different?

"Come on, old man," Jenny said. "Jean-Talon is waiting." She said it in English, no French accent, like she meant blue jeans and a bird's claw, and she tore at the air with a crooked finger.

* * *

Jean-Talon Market was its usual Saturday self. Mosaics of berries and greens and tropical fruits; middle-aged women, hair burgundy, clad in leather pants; maple vendors, their amber blood in leaf-shaped glass—Montreal was the veritable Garden of Eden. Lawrence inhaled the soup of scents—sausage and blue cheese, bread and lemons and lilies, the sweat and mould of nearly a hundred summers' worth of growth and spoilage—and Jenny's sweet blond hair, sprayed with a eucalyptus and lavender mix she'd created to ward off head lice. They're everywhere, she'd told him. I'm protecting myself from the plague. Wasn't he lucky to have this one-of-a-kind being at his side?

They made their way through the meandering, post-latte, post-coital crowd to the gelato stand. A dozen people stood in the lineup.

"I could go get started," Lawrence told Jenny. "This might take you fifteen minutes." He figured she would say no, since she couldn't imagine him out of sight in a public place, and would probably say, What kind of parent are you? Her tendencies were a direct inheritance from Vicki, but Jenny's centred more on survival. Although Vicki might disagree. She might say the sound of the fridge really was life-threatening.

But Jenny consulted her list. "I can see the egg man from here," she said. "Start on that and report back."

He smiled, a real smile, and it felt foreign, and very good. "Yes, ma'am."

He did an about-face and started marching away, until he heard Jenny call out, "Wait!"

He stopped and turned around; he'd almost made it.

"What flavour do you want?"

Lawrence opened his arms wide. "You choose. I like them all."

He was free. He was free.

The egg man carefully wrapped his dozen eggs in brown paper and string because he used the egg trays without built-on lids. This was a beautiful thing to Lawrence, this little oddity, marvellous that someone would still do this.

He had been checking back, visually, on Jenny in the lineup because she would be owling around, keeping her eyes on him. The line moved very slowly, which was natural; it was a difficult decision, choosing a flavour, and you couldn't go on colour. The mothy one, for example, was Lawrence's favourite. Noisette.

Beside the egg stand was a small flower booth selling the first of the sunflowers and dahlias. They weren't on the list, and Vicki didn't believe in cut flowers, but Lawrence was feeling free and good and brave, and he pointed to a bunch. The flower woman said, "Très bien, monsieur," and "Bonne fin de semaine," as she would to anyone. Today it felt personal.

Now with his flowers and eggs both wrapped like birthday gifts, he made his way back to Jenny. He couldn't see her right away, but the cutting board stand was in the way. No sign of her. Well, he would see her once he was around the throng of people at the maple syrup booth, maybe even through the line and waiting for him with two ice creams in hand. But no, when he made it, he still couldn't see her. He looked at the lineup again. She wasn't there.

Lawrence ran the twenty-five metres between himself and the gelato stand, holding the flowers and eggs tightly to his body, praying that she was just perfectly tucked in behind another person, or hiding from him on purpose.

"Jenny!" he cried, pushing his way through the throngs. He made their special whistle, a dash-dash-soar, once, twice, and waited for her reply. No reply came. When he was standing where she had been, where she should have been crouching down, fixing her sandal, scratching an itch, picking up a dropped quarter, he whistled again, and shouted again. Nothing.

"Have you seen my daughter?" he asked the people in line. "About this tall, wearing a pink puffy skirt, and um, a scarf, short blondish hair sticking up—"

The man standing behind where Jenny had stood said yes, she'd been right there. "She asked me to save her place," he said. "If I could."

Lawrence was nearly yelling now. "Where did she go? Where is she? Did she tell you anything?"

"No, just walked that way." He pointed toward the takeout food area, the picnic tables full of families.

Lawrence forced his way through the people waiting in line for crepes and smoothies and scanned ahead for Jenny. He hadn't asked the man if anyone was with her, or if she had followed someone, or if she looked scared. He couldn't go there.

Maybe she was sick. Otherwise she would still be in the lineup, singing to herself, watching Lawrence's every shopping move. But if she was sick, she might have gone to the bathroom. Aha! The women's washroom. But he was a man. He would have to wait. He couldn't wait.

He called into the bathroom for her, "Jenny! Are you in there? Jenny?"

A leather and burgundy woman came out and asked him in perfect English if he was all right.

"No, I'm not all right! I've lost my daughter."

"Oh, dear. What does she look like?"

Lawrence described Jenny again, and the woman's eyes widened when he mentioned the scarf with the holes in it she might be wearing over her face, but she said she would go back in and search.

"Thank you." Lawrence tried to keep his eyes on the gelato line, but the crowd was thickening, as if a nightmare's fog was descending, keeping him from everything he needed to see.

He'd been terrible. His cheek hot against the concrete block wall, he itemized how he'd made this happen. You wanted a break, you got it, buster. You are a horrible father. You should never have brought her here the day before she was about to see her mother. You knew she didn't want to come.

Oh, shit. Vicki would burn him to the ground.

What was taking that woman so long? Either Jenny was in there or she wasn't. He was just about to call in once more when his helper reappeared. She looked happy.

"She's in there, monsieur."

"Oh, thank God." Lawrence collapsed against the wall and closed his eyes. A second later he opened them. "Is she okay?"

"Well, she's in a . . . delicate position." The woman leaned in closer. He smelled garlic and coffee. "She's got her monthly visitor."

Oh, my God. He felt punched. "What do I do?"

The woman laughed. "Don't worry, I got her what she needed, for the moment."

"But—"

"Give her these." She pointed at his bouquet. "And be gentle with her. Treat her sweetly. La tendresse."

Lawrence tried to smile as he thanked her again. Gentle? He could be gentle with Jenny. He was *always* gentle with Jenny.

His mind leapt to Vicki. He was having trouble being gentle with her. He was confused. Relieved. Angry.

She should have warned him that this could happen, this, this sudden onset of menstruation. She should have given him a heads-up. How the hell was he supposed to know? He scrolled through his numbers to find her cell and hit the call button.

The words coming out of his mouth when Vicki answered his call would not be gentle. They would not be coming from a place of equanimity. And if she asked him in her newly modulated voice if he knew that anger was just a mask for fear? He would say that he did. Of course he did. And he would still be angry.

Jenny came out of the bathroom. She looked paler than normal, and she was no longer wearing her long johns or her scarf.

"Hi, honey," he said and flipped his phone shut. It had gone to Vicki's voice mail, the greeting a meditation gong. His legs felt like mush. "How are you feeling?"

Jenny didn't reply; she looked at him as though she didn't know him. She walked toward the gelato vendor.

"You still want ice cream? I mean, don't you?"

"Yes, I do," she said.

"Okay." They walked in single file until they reached the lineup. Everyone looked suspicious to Lawrence, as if Jenny was still missing and one of them had taken her.

He stood behind her, hoping she'd lean back into him like she usually did. But she didn't lean back.

"I can wait by myself," she said.

"No, no. I'll stay with you. I should have earlier, too."

Jenny turned around and looked at him, seriously. "Daddy, it's okay." She lowered her voice. "I'm a woman now."

Lawrence blushed. "Okay." He remembered the flowers. "These are for you." He held out the bouquet. "Um, congratulations?"

Jenny's face opened up, a sunrise entering a grey morning sky. "Oh, my God! Thank you, Daddy!" She clutched him in a fierce hug.

The leather lady had been right on the money. "Are you sure you'll be okay here?" Lawrence asked when she let him go. "I'll keep checking back—I mean—if you . . ." He shrugged. "You gave me quite a scare there."

"I'm sorry," Jenny said. "I just felt—I just had to go, right then."

Lawrence nodded. "We'll get you home soon. And get you whatever you need."

Jenny's sunny face turned dark, and within five seconds she was crying.

"What is it? A cramp? Do you want to sit down?"

She shook her head and tried to calm her sobbing. "I just, I just think I need her. I need Mom. She's supposed to be here for this kind of thing."

Lawrence pulled her back in for another hug. "I know. I know. You're totally right." He pressed his cellphone into her hand. "Call her and tell her that. And tell her brunch is now dinner, tonight. No excuses." Vicki had wanted a couple of days to readjust before coming to visit. Well, she wasn't going to get them.

"Okay," Jenny said, wiping her face on her sweatshirt sleeve. "Go get the rest of the stuff."

He did as instructed, rushing through as fast as possible, taking all the plastic bags the vendors offered to speed things up. When he stepped on a woman's toe, and heard her gasp, he pretended not to notice. He had another woman to look after.

＊ ＊ ＊

Lawrence made it back to Jenny in less than ten minutes. She was standing beside a garbage can, holding, and licking, methodically, back and forth, two cones of gelato.

"I got you lemon, too," she said. "Since I had to keep up with the drips."

"Thank you." He lifted up his bags. "All done." He waited for her plastic bag lecture, but it didn't come. "Let's sit and enjoy it before we head back home."

At one of the picnic tables, covered in syrup spills and empty sugar packets, Lawrence parked the groceries and patted the seat beside him. "We'll face out," he said, "so we don't have to look at this mess."

Jenny checked the back of her skirt before she sat down beside him. She smiled. "Okay."

"So," he said.

"She's coming. Tonight."

"Ah," Lawrence said. "Good news. Did you, um, tell her?"

Jenny nodded. "She's bringing me everything I need."

"Good," he said. "Great." What did the *everything* include? What did she need? How complicated *was* menstruation, anyway? And why did he not really know? He remembered brown paper bags in the bathroom cupboards when he was a boy, and asking his sister what pads were for. She'd told him they were for lining women's shoes, to keep them smelling fresh. He'd believed her for far too long.

"She's coming over soon, too," Jenny said. "Like in an hour or so. She might even beat us home."

Dammit! They had two metro lines to catch, followed by a ten-minute walk. Small wings of panic opened in his gut. The house was a mess. He hadn't washed the baking dishes from last night, and there was chocolate chip cookie dough flattened into the kitchen floor because he was the one who had stepped on it and left it there.

"She cried," Jenny said. "I think that's a good sign, don't you?"

Lawrence nodded. But would serenity, or joy, or forgiveness—whatever Vicki was feeling—would it be enough to make her blind or deaf? He hadn't admitted it, but he had enjoyed his months away from her hyper-vigilance. Not having to line the silverware up with the pattern on the tablecloth. Not keeping his voice down to a whisper when she was reading in the next room. Not needing to rinse the rice five times, or measure it to the exact top of the cup.

* * *

Vicki wasn't there when they got home. But a bouquet of flowers was on the doorstep—cosmos and daisies and a lush pink rose in the middle—snug in a tall Nutella jar.

"Ooh!" Jenny said. "More flowers!"

"Strange," Lawrence said.

"Mom probably dropped these off and then forgot something and had to go back to her . . . to . . . to wherever she's staying."

He let her think that. He unlocked the door quickly and hustled Jenny inside. He didn't want her to see him scanning Mia's yard or windows, even if it was just to check on her flower varieties. No use in checking, anyway; he already knew.

"Two bouquets in one day!" Jenny exclaimed. "This whole menses thing is *all right*." She started rummaging for vases under the sink.

"Why don't I do that while you go get ready for dinner? Maybe a bath?"

Jenny looked at him, a shocked face. "I can't," she whispered. She pointed at her abdomen.

"Oh. Well." Lawrence reddened. "Really? You can't? Not supposed to?"

She shook her head. "No heat allowed."

He racked his brain trying to remember if Vicki had followed this rule. He didn't know. "Okay," he said. "How about cleaning your room?"

She had spilled sequins and beads on her floor about a week ago, searching for a glass bead in the shape of a fish.

She sighed. "I guess." But it was a happier response than he'd become used to, and she robot-walked down the hallway.

Lawrence found the vases, arranged both bouquets of flowers, and looked around the kitchen for an empty surface they could sit on. Flower-perching spots should be the least of his concerns— the macaroni Jenny made two days ago was still in the pot, a congealed yellow brain. On the kitchen table, his newspapers from the past week were layered, newest on top, and in between he'd left toast plates and an unfinished game of Crazy Eights. He had to get to work.

By the time the doorbell rang, he had managed to scrape the dough off the floor, wash the dishes, and clear the table.

"I'll get it!" Jenny yelled and came running down the hall. Lawrence stayed behind as she flung the door open and called, "Mama! Bienvenue!" Then she started to cry again.

His wife was standing there, holding a cake box, a plastic shopping bag, and some kind of statue: a white woman with her arms raised over her head in a perfect circle. "Take this, Lawrence," she pleaded, handing him the cake. "It's so heavy I nearly dropped it."

He lifted the lid to peek inside. Black forest cake, white fluff on top, a circle of goopy cherries around the perimeter.

Vicki put the bag and the statue down beside her and locked Jenny in an embrace, rocking slightly from side to side. Jenny would be her height within two years.

His wife was home.

Lawrence felt winded. He left them in the hall and took the cake into the kitchen, sat down at the table and considered what it held. Flowers and cake: signs of celebration. He wasn't feeling it. He'd have thought that Jenny, of all people, would be mortified at this strange holiday in honour of blood. Ordinarily she pretended to faint when she cut herself. Or were they celebrating something else, too? A homecoming? Then he looked at the cake again, its shining red garnish.

"Cherries?" he said when she and Jenny came into the kitchen. "*Cherries*, Vicki?"

"What do you mean?" she said, but the look on her face told him she got the obvious reference to what he was most afraid of in the world: his daughter, a sexual being. Not his little girl any more, but a girl in the world. About to begin a part of her life that would involve things he wouldn't know about. And fertile. "Oops," she said.

"What's wrong with cherries, Daddy?" Jenny, red-eyed and sniffly, swiped a fingerful of whipped cream and a couple of glazed cherries and stuck them in her mouth. "It's delicious."

"Nothing's wrong, sweetie," Vicki said. "Now let's go into your room and see what I brought for you."

Lawrence followed them into the hallway.

Jenny's eyes widened when Vicki handed her the bag, bulky with packages, looking like a bag of gifts. Then her eyes closed. "Great," she said in a monotone. "How exciting."

"Come on. It's not so bad. And, this." Vicki turned back to the statue she'd left by the door. She looped her arm into Jenny's. "A moon goddess," Vicki said to Lawrence. "For our little woman."

Since when was Vicki like a buddy to Jenny? Since when did she smile like that?

Oh, that's right. Ever since she walked out and became a free agent, in search of nirvana. How she got to be the good guy was beyond him, and it made him angry, again. Surrender was all well and good, if you had the time, but it wasn't what you wanted in a parent. You wanted tenacity. You wanted strength. Who, out of the two of them, would pick up a car pinning Jenny to the ground?

He remembered the sound the Wii console had made as it hit the concrete at the bottom of the stairs and smashed. A Christmas gift to Jenny from them both that Vicki grew to hate. The synthetic music irritated her.

When he went back into the kitchen to start dinner, he could smell sweetness above the high notes of the cake's sugar and cream and red glaze. It didn't take him long to find it: the pink rose in the centre of Mia's bouquet. Ah, Mia. In this neighbourhood of three-storey walk-ups that boasted the highest per-kilometre density in

Canada, he'd had his share of wackos, winos, and the unwashed. She was the best neighbour he'd had in years. Lucky man. He tucked his nose in for a closer sniff.

* * *

A few minutes later, Jenny came out dressed like a regular person. A blue dress he hadn't seen before, little white flowers all over it, her hair brushed and pinned back with clips.

He waited to see her expression before commenting. "Looking good," he said.

She did a spin to make her skirt swirl. "Mom wants to know if you could go into my room for a second. Plus, if you haven't started cooking, she wants to take us out for dinner."

What the hell? The sabotage had begun. "Really?" He stood up and had to concentrate on keeping his fingers from becoming fists. "We just bought all this stuff."

"We could make it tomorrow, Daddy, like we'd planned. Or we could give her some to take with her. I mean, if she isn't— staying . . ." He could see that Jenny was going to cry again.

"I'll talk to her," Lawrence said, squeezing her shoulders. "Everything is going to work out." That was what regular people said to each other. Did they believe it? Even though Vicki was here, being a mother in a moment when Jenny needed her mother, asking him to talk in private—smiling—he was having trouble believing it. He kissed the top of Jenny's head. But kisses on the head, over hair, never feel like kisses should.

* * *

Jenny had cleaned up most of her beads, but a few of them pressed dents into Lawrence's bare feet as he walked across her room to the bed, by the window. She had the best view in the flat: a huge maple, leaves wide and open as faces, looking back in. He could see

Jenny's long johns and scarf drying on the clothesline. Who had done that? Time seemed to have slipped sideways on him.

Vicki patted the bedspread. "Sit," she said.

Lawrence pulled Jenny's swivel chair out from the desk instead. She was still smiling. A tattoo of a smile.

"Why a restaurant?" he asked.

"I thought it would save us all the trouble of cooking. And you know, to celebrate."

"We have a cherry-covered cake to help with that," he said.

"And lots of lovely flowers, I noticed," Vicki said.

Lawrence looked at the tree outside. "We were at the market."

"Lawrence," she said. "This is a big day for her. For us."

He looked right at her. "Why didn't I know? To expect it?"

She laughed. "Welcome to the life of a woman. You never know what you'll get thrown."

He ran his hands over his face, trying to rub in some calm, some patience. "But there had to have been signs?"

"Yes, Lawrence. She's been developing for years, in case you didn't notice. Sure, she's gotten it earlier than some, but it's within common range."

"Well, what do we do?"

"We don't *do* anything. I brought her enough supplies to last a few months, and showed her how to use them."

"But . . . I mean . . . what does all this mean? Miss Cherry Cake?" He stared at the goddess statue now on Jenny's nightstand: a small-breasted, wide-hipped woman, a spiral in the centre of, well, her centre.

"She knows all about sex, if that's what you're getting at," Vicki said mildly. "And she's still years away."

He thought about bringing up Jenny's penis question but decided against it. "And then what? Where will you be when things get really interesting?"

She sighed. "I don't know."

Lawrence looked at her. "You don't know?"

"I'm not ready yet. To make a decision. About us."

"Three months wasn't long enough?"

She closed her eyes. "I'm in a better state now. Happier. But I don't know how long that would last, if . . ."

"If you had to live with us."

She opened her eyes and looked at him. "I'm sorry, Lawrence. I just don't know right now."

He nodded and looked away. He felt cavernous, an empty warehouse. This was it; he was on his way to becoming an unmarried man. A single father. What he'd been practising at for the past three months. "Well then, we need to make some plans. Visitation, all of that."

"Okay," she said. She paused and took a big breath in through her nose, then let it out slowly through her glossy lips. Her hands were palms up, the tips of her middle fingers and thumbs touching. "I thought she could come and live with me now, in Mile End. You've had her for three months, and believe me, I wish that could have been different. But there were no kids allowed at the centre."

Her face was calm and serene as she said this, as if she were saying she might go take a shower. No kids allowed. No kidding. He'd never felt as off-centre as he did right then. He said, "No. She can't."

She breathed again, eyes closed. "I've already asked her," she said. "She's thinking about it. Especially when I told her how close we'll live to Figaro. You know how she loves that café. And it's not far from here—only a fifteen-minute walk."

He felt he would fly into a thousand pieces. All he'd been asking for, in his head, was a little break from Jenny, just a day or two a month. He couldn't lose her. Vicki couldn't have her. It wasn't going to be a battle about the kid. What about the marriage? Where had that suddenly gone?

"We could do some sort of rotation. It would give you more time alone, for your music."

"What are you talking about? Since when has Jenny been a problem for my music?"

"I know it's not easy, always having a child around." She paused. "You look tired."

"I'm fine." He rubbed his eyes. "I'm fine."

"Are you sure?"

He looked for Vicki's wedding ring. Not there. "What about you? Won't she get in the way of becoming transcendent, or whatever you call it?"

"Oh, Lawrence," she said. "I'm just trying to figure out my path, honey. My greater purpose."

"Well, is co-parenting on the list? *Honey?*"

Vicki took an even noisier breath in, then out. "Of course it is."

He used to be worried about other guys, with Vicki's sparkly eyes and appetite for change, but he'd been focusing on the wrong danger. It was the desire for enlightenment that had smitten her. If he had to fight that sort of suitor, he was weaponless.

Lawrence picked up the goddess, made from some sort of resin with a faux finish. What was this thing doing in his house? He ran his index finger around the spiral in the statue's centre, then realized what he was doing and set it back on Jenny's nightstand. His fingertip tingled. Was that supposed to happen?

"Isn't it powerful?" Vicki was giving him another tender smile. She wasn't tender; *he* was tender. A little more pressure on him and he would weep.

And yet, he would be pressured. There was no way out of this moment. "It's cheap," he said. "I can't believe you think it has any power at all."

The conversation might have continued in this manner, but Jenny came in. She handed each of them a piece of her puppy-edged paper. In her nearly illegible script, like doctor's writing, except in purple ink, she'd written three names: Doctor Goldstein, Doctor Bergeron, Doctor Reed. Phone numbers beside each of them.

"They're shrinks," she said. "Call them, and work it out." She looked like she'd been crying again. "Please. But not right now. I'm starving."

Vicki laughed as if nothing had just happened. "I always get that way when Aunt Flo comes a-calling."

"Mom!" Jenny said. "Don't say things like that. God, you're so bourgeois."

"Jenny, go slice the cake," Lawrence said. "We'll start with that."

"Really? Really?" She reached to the sky, asking for a high-five, and he gave her one before she bounded out to the kitchen.

"Dessert before dinner?" Vicki said.

"You're the one who wanted a party, remember?"

Vicki wiped at the dust on the headboard.

"I can't talk about this now," Lawrence told her. He stood up and walked toward the door.

"Fine," she said and looked down at the list. "Where on earth did she get these names?"

"Google," he said. "She's no dummy."

"Le gâteau!" Jenny called from the kitchen.

"Should we order in?" Vicki asked.

"No," Lawrence said. "I'm cooking what I bought today."

"Okay, but you don't seem to be in the best, um, state, to create a meal."

He glared at her. "I better go meditate, then."

Vicki smiled and shrugged. "It wouldn't hurt."

* * *

ABBA was wailing from the radio on top of the fridge. Vicki didn't move to turn it down, as she normally would have. She and

Lawrence stopped to stare at the table. Jenny had sliced the cake in three pieces, but not from the top down. Instead, she had divided it in layers onto dinner plates, separated it back into its original single layers. Her new blue dress had flecks of cherry and cream and chocolate all over it.

"The top is mine," Jenny said. "I stuck my finger into every bit of it. And neither of you want my germs."

Lawrence watched Jenny watching Vicki for a reaction. Jenny no doubt wanted to know how far she could take things, how much longer the calm around Vicki might last. He wanted to know, too. It was a good test, what Jenny had set up. In fact, it was brilliant.

In the rose-and-chocolate-scented air he and Jenny looked at Vicki, trapped in that small kitchen, her eyes darting around, still smiling that new smile. "Dancing Queen" blared its way into the picture as Jenny stood behind her bouquet of sunflowers, swaying to the music; she looked like a war bride getting married in her best dress. What was that idiom about necessity being the mother of invention? Lawrence had done what he'd had to do. He'd become the mother-father, and made it this far. But in this standoff, stare-down moment, despite losing his daughter today, and miraculously, finding her again, he felt a kick of energy return to him. He stood in front of the radio, to block Vicki from shutting the party down. She stepped toward him, smile atrophied, then changed her course. Vicki walked the three steps to the counter and picked up Mia's bouquet. She buried her face in it, seeking solace in the face of chaos, like any visitor might.

Damage

Mornings were heavy. Jim had time on his hands and didn't know how to spend it. This morning there had been a funeral in his dream, a problem with finding the casket of a relative he'd loved. He'd been wearing a decent suit, running all over town, and he awoke exhausted and worried. The day, so far, had brought no phone call to give him any news.

Maybe he was mourning the loss of news. No longer any letters, no phone calls, just an inbox full of stupid emails about the country's bad politics and deals on more junk he didn't need. What did he need?

Maybe it was nature. There was a wind strong enough to slam shut the windows that he'd opened to freshen up the place. Stuff built up in the night; whatever the body didn't need, it released during sleep. That was a lot of shit to remove. Last night, like most nights, he'd sensed a change in the air once Fran, his wife, fell asleep. He'd lain for hours with her beside him, snoring lightly, her back toward his back, and waited for sleep to take him, too.

Outside, Jim found a corner where he could set up his lounger out of the direct wind. The weather had been strangely hot during the past few days, so he was glad of the breeze, but the sun was still out, and he was also glad of that. All this gladness should have made him satisfied.

He lay in his chair and watched the clouds racing across a book-blue sky as if being hounded by salesmen. These clouds seemed to have internal desires, changing as they passed, from animal to gargoyle to spirals, a bit of pure blue above him before the next morphing creature came along. They made him feel useless, inert as a stick. He closed his eyes. Jim knew it was the wind against his eyelids, but it felt like the clouds were brushing him as they streamed past. Better if he kept an eye on them, to know where they were.

He heard someone yell, "Get out of the car." His neighbour, Carl. "Go and sit on the porch and do not move."

Then he heard whimpering.

Carl shouted, "Are you stupid?"

Crying.

"Go. Sit. On. The. Porch. *Now*."

Jim waited to hear a slap. Fran had told him that he would have to wait until there was something concrete to report before he called in a complaint. The system was designed to fix what was broken. What could be seen, like physical damage, damage that left nothing to dispute.

"*Owen!* For fuck sakes, did I not tell you to bring your bag in?"

Jim closed his eyes and concentrated on the wind. On clouds pressing in on his eyelids. On going deaf.

* * *

Jim's wife was "still in the market for a kid," as she liked to say. He knew that she thought this kind of teasing was funny, that if she made her longing seem light then he would lighten up, too, and they would get going. This was the thing: he couldn't come without pulling out. He'd tried—good God, he'd tried—but every time he was close, a bodiless face began to hover over Fran, like one of those baby angels with the big cheeks.

Not just any baby. The baby he'd pulled from the car just before the explosion, eight months ago. He hadn't thought about spinal cords or brains or anything other than getting the baby out. He'd seen the baby, he'd acted.

They told Jim the baby would've died anyway. Of course she would have; the car exploded. But she'd been alive in his strong arms and then he was running as fast as he could, away from the bomb of a car that was about to go off and toward a house with a big white porch.

He tripped. He fell. He fell on her.

✳ ✳ ✳

Carl and his wife had two kids and an ancient white dog they kept tied up to their back porch. The dog spent most days in the shade cast from the shed, in a hole he'd dug into the lawn, and barked whenever anyone passed, and Carl yelled whenever the dog barked. "Jasper! Shut up!" Jim heard the pattern at least a dozen times a day.

More recently the older boy had started yelling at the dog, too. Little voice, big voice, both of them carried easily over their chain-link fence, the back lane, and Jim's fence.

The neighbours lived kitty-corner across the shared back lane. Their windows were uncurtained, even at night. When Jim couldn't sleep, he liked to walk in the darkness, and every time he passed Carl's house, there were lights on, and Carl was in the dining room, sitting at a table, concentrating. It didn't matter what time, Carl was there.

So, insomnia was one excuse. He imagined a child could try a sleep-deprived person's patience. He knew what not-sleeping felt like, knew the sandy feeling in the brain, the cells responsible for common sense eroding with every wave of fatigue.

Money didn't seem to be the issue. Carl's house looked like it was trying to be Italian; they had the Tuscan colours, burnt orange, mum yellow, that deep ocean blue. They had a new boxy vehicle, the kind that was supposed to be both safe and good for the planet. Carl's wife wore nice clothes, on the rare occasions Jim saw her.

What was odd was that Carl didn't act like he cared about what people heard or saw. He wanted to be noticed, as if he were proud of it all, big man with the family and the house and the pretty wife. Like he had nothing to hide.

About three weeks ago, Jim had started keeping a journal of the things Carl said.

The kids and Carl had gone inside. All was quiet. Jim opened his eyes to a pair of hawk-eye clouds swirling past. He felt naked out there, stared at by a sky full of menace. The wind was overriding the sun to the point of him feeling cold. He would have to go in soon, and make some lunch, and put the morning behind him. He would write: *Called his son stupid. Said fuck sakes.* He had already filled four pages.

* * *

At 12:30 PM, Fran phoned. Fran's thing: she had her half-hour of chit-chat and lunch with the girls at work, and then called her useless husband to check in. Checking in meant asking how he'd slept, if he'd eaten breakfast, how he was feeling, and a question or two that changed from day to day: Would he like chicken for dinner? She could pick up a rotisserie bird on the way home. Did he want to go see a movie? Was it okay if she went to the gym straight after work?

He always made sure to switch on the radio before 12:30 so she'd hear the background noise. She didn't like the thought of him all alone in a silent house. She'd told him she would go crazy in all that empty space, all that quiet. He couldn't explain to her that silence was what he wanted, because she would get worried again. She would take it personally and think she was too noisy.

She *was* too noisy, but he couldn't hold that against her. Before, he'd loved the sound of her voice. He'd wanted to hear her singing in the bathroom while she put on makeup. Before, he was a regular husband who could carry on a conversation without crying or going mute. He was a man who'd worked. He was a husband who could make love to his wife and not see dead babies floating in the room.

Today she told him about a craft fair she was thinking about going to on the weekend. "They might have those handmade dishcloths we can't seem to find anywhere else."

He knew she loved him. She wanted to involve him; that was the prescription. "Good idea," he said into the phone, without a trace of sarcasm or himself in it at all.

* * *

After lunch—a sensible bowl of tomato soup and a slice of brown toast—Jim went into the backyard to check on his garden. He'd never been the type, but gardening had turned to therapy, to sticking things into the muck and seeing what good came out of it. He had to admit there was a thrill in watching the first leaves emerge from the soil in his little raised bed or in the flower beds alongside the house. He liked to get down on his knees to get a really decent look at the pea shoots, their leaves still tucked tight against the stems. Today the onions were at least two inches tall, which made him feel better than he had all morning. A lightness was starting to replace that stony weight.

"Get your goddamned shoes off my goddamned pants," Carl yelled.

Jim stood up in time to see Carl carrying his younger son toward their vehicle. He was carrying the child as if he were a bag of stinking garbage. Jim caught a glimpse of the boy's face before Carl shoved him into his carseat. The kid was grimacing.

"Wait for me!" the other boy called, racing around the car.

"Owen!" Carl said. "Get back in the yard until I tell you."

"But you'll leave without me!"

"I wish I could. You're such a little shit."

Owen started to cry.

"Oh great," Carl said. "Another baby. Just get in the fuckin' car already."

Jim walked back toward the house before Carl noticed him. The seedlings around the other side of the house needed some attention.

* * *

Reframing the situation was supposed to help. Jim tried this trick from therapy, now and again: he wrote down what had happened and how he felt, and then he tried to spin the experience into a positive. But when he tried, *I killed that baby*, he couldn't find anything positive. Or else he took the present tense approach—*I am here, this is now, nothing else exists*. None of it worked. That was the thing about brains: they were as stubborn and unpredictable as drunks.

Maybe that was Carl's problem. Or was it drugs? Jim had been given so many prescriptions since the accident that he could've raked in some serious cash as a salesman. Not one pill had worked, at least not in the five-day trials he'd allowed each of them. Overall, he felt no worse just letting history and time battle it out.

He reframed in other ways. He put Carl and his family in olden-day situations, for example, to see if he was overreacting. Would they be shouting if they were all piling into a covered wagon? Jim tried to imagine kids from a hundred years ago, and wondered if complaining had been an option. Then again, parenting was a different beast back then, too—children were farmhands, servants, mouths to feed so they'd take care of the livestock at dawn.

He put Carl in a hundred different scenarios, trying to find a place where he would fit. Prison guard came up roses, or overseer of slaves at a diamond mine, a punishing sun turning everyone mean.

Jim also tried to imagine a situation in which those boys were in the wrong. But even if they wrote on the walls with their own shit, or pulled the antique china down from the shelves, didn't parenting come down to supervision, rules, boundaries?

Boundaries. Man, he'd never used that word before. Fran would like his learning, the way she loved to see him caring for the garden. She'd never seen that side of him, she said.

It was sexy, she said.

He guessed she'd thought he was only his work self—when he was working—and the working man had not been able to show anything close to what he gave to his plants. Tenderness was not a part of the municipal worker's world. Gentleness was something seized upon, laughable; his job-site self had been as leathery as his skin, out there all day, roadside, keeping the whole city running. Keeping the roads as safe as possible.

The baby's name was Kaitlin. Her mother's car had met another head-on. No one from the accident was still alive.

* * *

When Fran got home, his heaviness had returned. She found Jim in the spare room with the journal in his lap, the growing list of Carl's infractions.

"A bad Carl day?" she asked him.

He nodded.

She sighed. "We could move, you know."

He looked at her.

"It's not impossible," she said. "You know he's not going to move, and we can't live like this. Plus, that's the good part about renting. We can pick up any time we like."

"You've thought about this," he said. So had he, but every time he did, the thought of leaving his garden kept him from getting too far down that road.

She nodded. She blushed a little, even. "I just get so upset by all of this, and I don't know what to do, so I . . . search Craigslist, seeing if there's anything better."

"They don't put who the neighbours are, do they?"

She pulled her lips in, the way she did when she was holding something back. "No, they don't."

"Let me call someone," he said. "Someone has to help. He just can't get away with this."

Fran didn't want to meddle. Didn't want to stir the pot. She wasn't at home, listening the way he was. She only heard a fraction of what went on.

What he wanted to do was watch time-lapse videos of plants growing, over and over. There was goodness in this pastime, being mesmerized as each plant reached for the sun. It was inevitable: they were meant to strive toward light. Their cells went about their business freely, no parents to steer them the wrong way, to mess anything up.

Some days, what Jim saw in those videos made him cry. Every kind of plant he watched moved up from the earth in a slow, waving dance. The petunias had made him sob once, their blooms opening and closing like trumpets of hope. The tomato plant responded to water so dramatically, it was abusive to keep it away; when the plant was dry, it stopped growing. The plant just stopped and waited.

Maybe some people could do it, bring babies up the right way. Maybe parenting did involve studying, although he found that hard to believe. Shouldn't raising a child be innate? Shouldn't it be second nature, animals bringing up their own? Survival of the species, all that?

More than anything, Jim was afraid of messing everything up.

But children were resilient, weren't they? He'd seen that before: a young girl with a double leg cast had crawled past him on the ferry, on her way to getting her hip dysplasia corrected, and her father had seemed unfazed. Jim saw young kids with glasses, too, and shaved heads from lice, and gleaming heads from chemo. They survived way more often than they didn't. The odds were with them, because of age and their ability to bounce back—the imperative to keep living. A tree was the same: it could grow around a pretty substantial gash, callous over, just keep growing, as long as its roots were intact.

＊ ＊ ＊

Jim awoke the next morning to the dual alarms of screaming and barking. Nothing new. But this morning, Fran had already gone to work, and he'd slept in—and the screams from across the back lane were louder. His heart felt like it was already at a hundred beats a minute before he even moved a muscle.

"I'll do it," he heard Carl shouting. "One more word and I'm doing it!"

The boy—or boys—didn't answer. He heard bawling. A syllable. A few more. Nothing recognizable as English.

The day was already hot; Jim had been sweating, drooling, dreaming of a day from when he was a greasy teenager, cooking French fries. Shake, dump, scoop, load, cook, shake, dump . . . There had been satisfaction in the routine, even though his acne had grown worse and the kitchen was hotter than Hades—

He heard a chainsaw. He leapt from bed and grabbed a pair of shorts and was at his back fence in twenty seconds.

Carl was about to cut down a tree. The one that held the treehouse, the tire swing. He couldn't hear the boys crying over the saw, but he could see them, sitting on the back porch, watching their father do surgery on their childhood.

He himself had done nothing to stop this from happening. Whether it'd been wrong or right to wait it out, he'd done nothing—

Jim opened his gate and ran across the back lane.

Carl looked like hell, unshaven and haggard, as if he hadn't slept in days. He'd cut off one limb—a non-essential limb—and it was lying at his feet.

Jim pointed at the chainsaw, motioned for Carl to turn it off with a hand slicing his throat.

"What?" Carl yelled.

"Turn it off a sec!"

The boys stared, faces wet and puffy, eyes wild, bodies shaking. The older one—Owen—grabbed his little brother and hugged him. The dog kept pacing and barking, straining against his collar.

Carl turned off the saw, held on to it with one hand. "Yeah?" He looked in Jim's general direction but not at his face.

"Hey, man." Jim tried to smile but the smile wouldn't come. "Tough morning?"

Carl's face was covered in sweat. "Jasper!" he yelled. "Shut the fuck up." The dog stopped for a few seconds, then started up again.

"Gonna be hard to regrow this," Jim said. "Pretty good shade tree."

Now Carl looked directly at him. Jim flinched. Beyond the man's dead eyes, beyond the grimace and the grime, Jim recognized what he saw. Desperation. A lot of pain. The same thing he faced every day.

But what could he do? Reach out, touch Carl, and say, Hey, look at us, buddy, we're in the same place, doing things we don't want to do, hurting the ones we love because we're suffering inside? No. His tenderness had no place here. Or did it?

The last time he'd tried to help someone, he'd killed a baby. But Carl had a chainsaw, and those boys were about to be shattered, again.

The boys were staring at him. The dog, too.

"Carl," he said. "Man." He put his hand on Carl's shoulder, the muscles, hot and alive. He heard the chainsaw hit the ground. When Carl's fist reached for his face, Jim felt it coming. He'd been waiting a long time.

Crossing Over

"I've got a favour to ask you," Gwen said. "Even though you've already done so much just by coming down here." She chewed on her cheeks as if her teeth belonged to a fish. Nibbling herself from within, like those goldfish Roy had seen in one of his wife's magazines—they used them in pedicures to eat dead skin off the feet.

Roy gave the slightest nod. Obviously his sister was still not back to her old self.

"Fluffy's Canadian, as you know," Gwen said. "Born in the Okanagan. I want to take him back to his native soil."

Roy's expression soured. "Oh, no."

"I have a plan," she said, brows high.

He held up his hands. "If it involves me taking a dead cat across the border, then I'm not interested."

The crying began. "But I promised!"

"You promised who?"

"Fluffy!"

"Oh, Lord." She was worse off than he'd thought. "The poor cat's gone, Gwennie. He won't know where he's buried."

"Exactly," she said. "We don't know what happens after we die, do we? Well, what if we rise out of our graves and live again? Wouldn't it be better if we knew where we were?"

Roy thought about this logic for a moment. He thought about Marjorie, his wife of forty years, resting, hopefully in peace, just a few kilometres from home in White Rock, in a park-like cemetery. "But wouldn't Fluffy prefer to be close to you? If he does . . . return?"

Gwen looked at him like he was the mad one. "Yes, but I'm not dead yet. And when I am, I'm going back to Canada, too."

"I thought you liked it better here."

She sighed. "I do. But that's not the point. I was born in Canada, and I'm to be buried there."

That was a heads-up—yet another job for Roy. "I can't take a dead cat across the border," he said, though he had no idea if what he said was true. Then a bright thought came. "Ashes, though. Yes—what about that, Gwen?"

She looked horrified. "You want me to burn him up. You want a . . . a . . . box of ashes to reconstitute itself into a cat on the next level?"

She'd been playing too many computer games, or consulting TV psychics. "Well, no, but I'm sorry. I'm still not doing it."

Oh, the wailing, then. She lost it and ran upstairs. Roy had to get outside, away from her stuffy house, Fluffy's hair on everything. He had to go home. He would pour on the sympathy a little more, go to Powell's Books, stock up on novels and a golf book or two, play a round with Gwen's neighbour Frank, and leave after dinner. Get out of Portland—land of doors, if you spoke French. The door to leave was fully open. He could be through all of Washington by midnight, cross the border quickly, be home by 1:00 AM. Not far off his typical bedtime: he was one of those rare geezers who could actually stay awake past nine and sleep in past six. It wasn't good for his golf schedule, since most of the old farts were on the course by seven.

He tried to live a balanced life, to keep the loose ends tied and the holes filled. At least, the little holes. The Marjorie hole was not easily filled. How could it be? Four decades together. It felt like the hole in the ozone. And Gwen? Not a loose end he enjoyed dealing with—a sister lonely as a lighthouse, all by herself in Oregon. Truly alone now, with Fluffy gone. It was going to be a long year ahead.

He heard the bath water running. Roy tapped on the bathroom door.

"Hey, sis," he called. "You okay?"

Nothing.

He knocked again. "Gwen?"

"I'm taking a bath, Roy. Use the other toilet."

"No, I don't—I'm just going to Powell's, okay? Then to play a round with Frank. "

"Fine. Lock the front door."

"Dinner at five?" Roy asked. "My treat?"

She didn't reply.

He would get her a box of good chocolates. Or maybe a book on grieving. Something about losing your best friend. Roy knew what that was like. But he was okay now, wasn't he? Well, good enough. He hadn't needed any books. Or if he had, no one had given him one.

* * *

Books purchased; balls hit; beer consumed. All in all, a decent day. But when Roy came back to Gwen's place, with pizza, book bag, and grocery store Chardonnay, he couldn't find her. He set his treasures down and found Gwen's body on the living room floor, eyes open.

"Gwennie!" he cried, then rushed to kneel at her side.

She blinked at him and reached her hand in front of her, as if sweeping the sunlit air.

"Can you speak?" He shook her shoulders. "Did you fall? What's my name?"

"Meow," she said. "Meeeeooooow."

"Gwen." Roy jostled her a little more. "What's going on?"

She continued to paw at nothing. "This was Fluffy's favourite place to lie," she whispered. "And all this time, I never knew what the fuss was about. But look! It's the dust floating. All along, he was watching the beautiful dust." Then she curled up onto her side and started purring.

"Gwen," Roy said sharply, now on his feet. "I bought you something today. Come out into the kitchen."

"Meow?"

"Like a human. Come on, now."

She did as he asked. Gwen had needed his guidance before—the time she wanted to leave a burning letter in her boyfriend's mailbox after she caught him cheating on her, the time she decided to quit high school and hitchhike down to California with a hundred bucks to her name. She'd listened to him back then, too; perhaps she was a little flighty, but at least she was compliant.

Once she was sitting down at the table, he gave her the book he'd found: *How to Let Go and Move On after a Loved One Crosses Over*. She took it from him, still mute.

"Might be useful," he said. "Now how about a glass of vino with your pizza?"

Gwen nodded, already leafing through the book. Maybe he'd hit the nail on the head.

While Roy chatted on about his day during the meal, she said nothing. Gwen just ate and drank and read little bits from the book, then stared into space. The sound of both of them chewing made Roy feel queasy; it reminded him of their mother. Their father always said she had exceptionally thin cheeks; he used to cover his ears when she chewed.

Finally Gwen spoke, interrupting Roy's monologue about the bad shape the putting greens were in. "I feel like ice cream."

"Sounds good. Got any?" Had that been a suggestion in the book?

"No. But there's that store two blocks away."

"Let's take a walk," he said. "You could use the fresh air."

"I can't. I've got a bad blister on my foot."

Roy sighed. "Okay, I'll go. Any flavour in mind?"

"Something caramel. No nuts."

Uh-huh. Enough of those already.

* * *

Gwen had moved down to Portland when she was in her forties, deep in an affair with a man who'd told her she was a goddess. Then, after marrying her and eating through her money like a termite, he left her for another goddess, and she was stuck in the United States with a great waitressing job and no love. Roy had tried persuading her to return to Canada, but it hadn't worked: she always said she had even less to come home to than what she'd be leaving. Not that he wanted her close by, by any means; he was thinking about the health insurance and whom she'd come to if anything went wrong. Luckily she'd been healthy enough, up until now. Now she was just being ridiculous.

But still, he went to the store for her. He was back within fifteen minutes, and found her in the living room, watching television. Good girl. Move on.

"I'm heading home after this, if that's okay," he said lightly, finishing his bowl of ice cream. "Better to go when the traffic's good."

"Okay," Gwen said. She smiled serenely at Roy and then back at the talk show on TV. That was the first smile he'd seen all weekend. He felt good, leaving her, like a decent brother, helping as much as he could. He tucked a hundred-dollar bill in her coffee canister before he packed up his car and aimed for the border.

* * *

The drive up I-5 was uneventful. Except for a stop in Olympia to get coffee, it was straight through to Canada. As predicted, the border lineups were short. Once the guard waved him through with a "Welcome home, sir," he felt more at ease. It was always like this, even though he liked the States well enough. Something to do with national pride, and the lack of personal firearms, but mostly it was the distance from Gwen. That line between countries was a decent fence, a good arrangement. Each had a country to themselves.

Was it mean to think of his only living relative in this way? Or was it par for the course after a lifetime of weirdness and demands on his time? She'd been a fussy child, given to insane fits of jealousy, and this continued once they were adults. Roy had been a successful owner of a hardware store while she had nothing to fall back on, but she'd made her choices and so had he, and he'd said as much, more than once. When their parents died, though, he was all she had, as far as family went. He'd been luckier than Gwen in this regard, too; he had Marjorie's family to call his own.

This was his train of thought when he hit the raccoon, just a few kilometres from home. By the time he circled back to check on the poor thing, it was too late to do anything but drive away. Another statistic, another victim of territorial wars. Humans were winning by a long shot. If Marjorie had been with him, she'd have told him the story—again—about the time she ran over a fisher up north, in the Sixties, and how she hadn't seen one of those animals ever since. He never knew why she'd want to see another one: she'd turned around to look at the dead animal and nearly had her ankle bitten when it snarled back to life right in front of her. He missed her stories, even after a dozen retellings.

Roy was exhausted by the time he pulled into his parking spot. He left his luggage and golf clubs in the trunk, and after a quick splash of milk and Baileys, he fell into a solid sleep.

✳ ✳ ✳

The phone woke him at seven the next morning.

"Thank you," said Gwen.

"For what?"

"For coming. For the book, and for the visit."

"You're welcome." He lay back down, his head foggy. "Is that why you called?"

"Yep," she said. "That's all. What are you doing today?"

Roy yawned. "I just woke up."

"More golf?"

"Yeah, most likely."

"Good for you. Well, I won't keep you."

She hung up before he could say goodbye.

Long distance used to be way more expensive, Roy thought. Too bad that had changed.

✶ ✶ ✶

Roy got up, did his thing, called his golfing buddy Stan, and made a plan for a round at ten. There was an odd smell in his car when he started it, but then he remembered the raccoon. He'd take it through one of those deluxe car washes on the way home.

Stan was waiting for him, cart already rented. He drove them both over to get Roy's clubs from the car. When Roy popped the trunk, the smell was worse.

"Lord," Stan said. "You got a dead body in there?"

"I hit a raccoon last night." Roy reached for his golf bag. Half the clubs slid out before he could pull it out of the trunk. It felt heavier than usual.

"You feel okay?" Stan asked. "You're not stroking on me, are you?"

Roy did not feel okay. He pulled the bag out and removed the rest of the clubs.

Below them lay a familiar-looking book: *How to Let Go and Move On.*

Below that, a thick white plastic bag with a note taped to its top. An address in his sister's loopy script for a place called Shady Pastures.

Roy sat down on his bumper. "Shit," he said. "She did it anyway."

"What is it?"

"You don't want to know."

"Well, can we still play a round?"

Roy did not know how he was going to get the smell out of his car, let alone after another few hours of heat. "Go on without me," he said. "Seems I've got a job to do."

* * *

He found the street he needed on the map in the glovebox. It wasn't more than three miles. As he drove, he called his sister on his cellphone, despite the fact that he didn't want her to know that number.

"You found him," she said.

"You've got some nerve."

"He was my baby," she said. "I just want to make sure he's taken care of."

Why was this his job? Marjorie had given Roy instructions for her funeral and burial, and had even written her death announcement out on the back of a prescription bag. It was a good thing; he'd been practically comatose. She was the planner of the family. Planning just seemed to naturally fall to the women he knew; Gwen was no exception to this pattern.

Before he lost his cool, he had to remind himself of the tragedy: her only love was wrapped in plastic in the trunk of his car. In half an hour, it would all be over and he could catch an afternoon round if it didn't rain.

"Okay," he said to Gwen. "I'll call you when it's said and done."

"I'm going to light some candles right now," she said. "Oh, and Roy?"

Her thanks would not be enough of a payment for this, but it was better than nothing. "Yeah?"

"Make sure they bury him on his back. That's how he used to sleep."

* * *

Roy checked out the pamphlets at Shady Pastures before speaking to anyone at the front desk, but he was still in shock over the prices. No, he would not be needing the complete package including a bronze paw, a memorial service, a gold-plated plaque, and the release of a hundred butterflies.

He decided on the "Simply Passing Through" option, which included a canvas bag and a bouquet of flowers on the gravesite. He brought Fluffy to the back door and tried to leave.

Oh, not yet, sir, they told him. We need someone from the family to witness the burial, and you need an appointment. But he was in luck, they said. They could do it immediately; there had been a cancellation from someone who still couldn't bear to put their diabetic ferret down.

And so he stood by the small hole in the ground—with Gwen on speakerphone after some strong encouragement from the director to include the bereaved for closure—as the burial of Fluffy took place.

* * *

Just before she passed away, Marjorie had told him that golf would get him through the worst of it. He'd believed her. It had seen him through a few rough patches, and she'd been there when over the years he'd said to whomever would listen, *If I didn't have golf, I'd be dead.* What a dolt. As if golf had carried him through losing his store to fire and rebuilding again, or the skin cancer scare, or the murmuring depression that set in once he retired. It was Marjorie. She'd just said *golf* to give him something to focus on, the way in the game itself you have to zone in on one thing only—getting that tiny ball across all that land and into the hole. And what for? Just a way to pass a bit of time in his long and lonely days without her.

Roy got back into his stinking car and hit the button to open every window. He ran the car through the first automatic car wash he found and then, too tired for golf—his buddies wouldn't believe his story, anyway—he headed for home. Then he changed his mind and headed for Marjorie.

At a roadside stand, he bought a bunch of dahlias, her favourite, although the ones she'd grown had been more vibrant, puffier.

He placed the flowers in the vase he kept at the front of their joint headstone, moved it from its position in the centre so the blooms would cover his name and let hers show. Then Roy used his fingers to rake the stray leaves from the grass above where she lay. He just wanted to sit down with her and talk. Who was the weird one now?

He'd brought Gwen's book with him from the car. To protect his golf pants from grass stains, he set it down on the plot and sat his old bones on top of it. With his back resting against Marjorie's name on the headstone, Roy began, in a shaky voice, to tell her about his day.

Pilgrim

When I decided to go to Arizona, Warren wasn't too happy about it.

I applied for a course in Sedona on angel reading, and when I got accepted, he kind of flipped. Why didn't you tell me? And I was all like, I didn't think you'd mind, and he said, Shit, girl, it's our life you're talking about, and I said, I know. I want to become a better person. Then he said, Aren't we trying to build something here, Lacy? And I said I needed to get realigned, and he told me I wasn't a car, needing its tires rebalanced, and I said, Well, I kind of like that metaphor.

Sedona's a centre for tuning in. I needed to expand my chakras, flush my channels, tune into the universe. Warren used to think it was cute, the way I believed in all this stuff, but then he went sad and mopey when I told him he should try to save his sexual energy instead of always spend, spend, spend. I was just trying to make him a stronger man.

He left our place in Peterborough and came back two days later, wearing a baseball shirt and sneakers, smelling like Taco Bell. Go, he said. Do what you like.

* * *

I thought about the moon a lot. I followed this astrologer on the west coast of BC, receiving her daily text updates about what to do or what not to do based on what was going on with the moon. People were under the lunar spell, she wrote; every earthling went through each day pulled by lunar strings. One day might not be a good day for real estate or financial planning—moon in Scorpio—but once the next morning came, bam! Buy that house.

I'd never looked for that kind of settling down. I was just passing through, as they say. In Sedona, I saw three Just Passing Through bumper stickers. My kind of place, if ever there was one.

The fact was, I didn't know where I belonged. My parents—military people—pulled me across the country and back a few times during my childhood, and I never found my soul home. I thought maybe Arizona was the place, but even after being there for two weeks, I still wasn't able to feel one bit of difference in my energy fields. Every day, at the ordained best times, I went to the airport vortex, sat cross-legged near the twisted juniper trees, and imagined every channel opening. All I felt was sunburn and red ants biting my butt.

I believed we were at the cusp of a new era. Life as we knew it was about to change, and the suffering would soon be over. What kept me sane was listening to other people like me. Seekers. Pilgrims. Carriers of the light. There were so many amazing webcasts out there that I spent most of my day tuning into interviews and guided meditations online when I wasn't in class at the Harmonic Healing Centre, learning how to sense the angels that surrounded us.

One morning, after yoga on my tiny deck overlooking the incredible valley of red-orange rock below, I tuned into one of my favourite sites and clicked on their latest podcast.

You will not see this on mainstream television, the show host said. **Censorship is alive and well in the United States and we are all test subjects in the experiment of how a government can keep their people in the dark. Breakfast cereals, chem trails, fluoride, vaccines, fast food, concentrated juices. You've been manipulated, folks. But it's not too late!**

I loved podcasts; I could pause them whenever I wanted to make myself a superfood smoothie. Even ten minutes of triangle pose and Savasana, the corpse pose, and my appetite was gigantic. That day, I added goji berries and some local herbs that were meant to increase psychic awareness, then settled into my papasan chair and pressed play again.

The host announced incredible news: nosebleeds had begun to affect a large percentage of residents in a New Mexico town. We're going to look into this strange happening and attempt to get to the bottom of it.

First, let's talk to a few of the people affected by the phenomenon.

This is Reuben, aged sixteen. "I think I was one of the first. The blood just started to pour onto my desk. I thought maybe I'd been thinking too hard. Sometimes my teachers tell me I overthink, you know, and although I knew it was scientifically unlikely, that's what I thought, too. Anyway, the blood missed my chemistry book, but once I felt the blood, I didn't do so well. Because you know, when you touch your own blood, you're basically inside your own body. I'd never had a nosebleed before. I didn't know how much blood could come out of me. Apparently I fell off my chair and passed out on the floor."

And Noel, fourteen. "I'd just climbed up into a tree in my back-yard, to spy on my sister and her friends. Usually she didn't even know I was there, but not that day. I felt the blood start pouring from my nose, and I hit my head on the limb above me. The yelling kind of gave me away. When I told my sister I was bleeding, she said, 'Not enough!' But I kept on bleeding, and she and her friends all screamed when they saw my bloody hands and shirt."

Deb, the mother of Sadie, eleven, was awakened by her daughter crying and holding her hand to her face, blood running between her fingers. "I was in bed, and grabbed the closest thing—my husband's T-shirt—and I told her to press it to her face. I can never remember if it's don't tilt your head back or don't tilt it forward. Seems they're always changing these pieces of advice. Anyway, Sadie asked me, 'Am I dying?' and I told her, No, of course not, it's just a part of growing. Then we went into the hallway and saw the trail from Sadie's bedroom into mine. She started wailing then, I tell you. 'I don't want to die!' I had to give her a sedative to calm her down."

Doug, eighteen, was playing basketball with his friend, Chum, when his nose started spilling its guts. "I'd just sunk a basket when I could taste blood. 'Oh, shit,' I said, and I like pinched my nose shut and ran to the water fountain to wash off. I really freaked out the little girl there, filling up her sand pail. It wouldn't stop, you know? It just kept pouring out, so I went to the walk-in clinic down the street, and I really freaked them out, too."

All of this happened last week. As you may have gathered, it's been affecting the young people first, but we have reports of adults succumbing as well. And, as you might expect, there are many theories, the link to food getting the most press. But when we come back after the break, we'll look at what communities are doing to manage the cases, and we'll talk with a man who's got another theory about all of this blood.

Gah. The idea of all that blood made me feel nauseous. Or it might've been the wheatgrass or herbs. Too much detoxification? Too much awareness of what my gut was trying to process? I unfolded my body from the chair, took a few Tums, and went back to listen.

And so this brings us to the next part of our show, where we ask the big questions: Why is this happening to this small community? And what can be done?

I was sitting on the edge of my seat, looking at the blue sky, the red rock. The podcaster interviewed Mr. Jones, from an organization called Lunar Hoax. "The moon never changes," he said. "Ever notice that?" I wasn't sure that statement was true, but he went on to say that Lunar Hoax believes the moon isn't all that it's cracked up to be. He wanted us all to doubt the moon.

"So what you're asking is, is the moon, in fact, a moon?"

"That's correct."

"Well, what do you think it is? Or might be?"

"We at Lunar Hoax believe that it is a satellite-like formation, a built object. We believe it is not simply a giant chunk of rock, in orbit around Earth, but a manufactured entity."

The host paused. "A man-made moon."

"No. Not man-made. Alien-made. We believe that it was created thousands of years ago as a means to control earthlings, and it's a hub from which they operate to this day."

"So, all this time, we've been worshipping a false moon? We walked on a satellite? Wolves howl at a space station?"

"Yes. That's what I'm saying."

"Wow. Now, I know many people will ask this: what about the tides?"

"A means of controlling seaside populations."

"Women's . . . cycles?"

"Yes, the aliens want to manage us in untold ways."

"Madness?"

"I assure you, it's not—"

"No, full-moon madness."

"Oh, yes. Well. That's what happens to those who've been abducted before. The full moon reminds them and they feel . . . a bit crazy."

I knew that feeling. Abduction? I lay down in Savasana, contemplating my situation. Aliens lived among us, Mr. Jones said. People pouring out blood was an alien control tactic.

"Have you ever"—and at this the host's voice dropped—"encountered one?"

"Not to my knowledge. But they are here, among us. And yes, I'm sure I have seen one, even if I don't remember. And so have you."

"Fascinating. Well, then. Maybe the ones who aren't bleeding are, in fact, not of this earth."

"Quite possibly. We just don't know."

I had to pause it there and walk around. Wow. That stuff got me so amped up! If Warren had been there, we'd have been walking around with the silver deely boppers from our New Year's party on our heads because he would've been having a field day with it all. Not that he made fun of everything I believed in, but that stuff would have sounded pretty crazy to him. Then he would have taken me to bed and called me his little alien, his coffee skin stunning against the white sheets. My pasty tone never could compare. Even in Arizona, my skin just turned pink and peeled.

But love isn't a colour. What got me with Warren was the air around him: it seemed to fizz a little. Some kind of force field I could not resist. And kindness! He gave me two gorgeous eggs—one of green glass and the other of blue and white marble. One day I was going on about the moon not being round but oval, more like an egg, and there he was, the next day, with these gifts. He was that kind of man.

His aura, of course, was that force field I'd been picking up. That's what started me on the way to thinking about all of this Sedona stuff. Opening up. Ah, the innocence of my first encounter. The first little step.

The podcast moved onto the next section: callers.

"I'm worried about this," the first caller said. "It's a recipe for civil war. Think about it. If this thing spreads, it might be neighbour against non-bleeding neighbour. You're gonna see fake blood recipes flying all over the Net, just so people can survive."

The host asked her if she had any theories about its source.

"Oh, probably hormones. Isn't that why we're all messed up?"

"Let's go to our next caller, Bob from Idaho. Hello, Bob."

"Howdy."

"So, Bob. What do you believe about the source of this bleeding?"

"He's right."

"Beg your pardon?"

"Jonesy, there. He's right. They're out to keep us under their thumbs. Or whatever it is they've got dangling from their arms."

"I see. And . . . have you seen one, yourself?"

"Well, now, I'm not sure, like Jones said. They're here, and in good disguises. I don't think it's the non-bleeders, though. But I know they're here."

"So. What do we do?"

"Well," drawled Bob from Idaho, "if y'all see a spacecraft, run the other way. If they can convince a whole planet to believe in the moon, they've got a lot more they want to do to us."

The podcaster said goodbye to us earthlings. He said, "Love your neighbours, whether they bleed or not."

I lay on my floor and tried to imagine a whole town bleeding from their faces. It made me ill; I scooted into the bathroom just in time. But maybe it was my precious moon, being talked about in such a way that had me feeling sick. I mean, sure, *aliens*, of course they were out there, but the moon as a disguised alien spaceship? It was deeply disturbing.

✳ ✳ ✳

Shortly after this, the problem started to spread. At first it was just the young people in a few other towns close to the first, but it only took a day for it to jump the state line and affect all ages. Within a week, the whole country was suffering. Not everyone bled, but the outcome was pretty massive. You couldn't get a bottle of iron supplements for less than forty bucks, and tissue prices tripled.

At first I wasn't worried. I was in Sedona, surrounded by vortices.

I was drinking potions of every colour, learning to see angels, standing on my head daily. I wasn't American.

The theories came by the thousands. It was the meat: the blood was running because we'd killed too many beasts. It was the milk: cattle hormones mixing with human, bound to eventually cause trouble. The gigantic glasses of milk once prescribed to and enjoyed by bulking-up teens were exchanged for soda. The environment got a bad rap: global warming, of course, because blood flowed better with heat.

The US government created policies. No driving while bleeding. Disposal of bloody tissues in specific incinerator bags only. Spitting of blood was absolutely prohibited, ditto vomiting, even though it was a common reaction.

People began to walk under umbrellas when outdoors because the sun seemed to make it worse. Mostly they stayed in, distraught and queasy, as immobile as possible, heads held stiffly so the movement didn't trigger another jag. Schools kept PE to a minimum, and they did away with projects, chemistry, home economics, and the more strenuous subjects like trigonometry and world history. All of that seemed to tax the brain too much, which brought on bleeding. Hospitals were plugged with bleeders at the beginning, but that got better after another ruling came down. If you had bleeding symptoms alone, you had to go to an EMC—an Epistaxis Management Centre—where hastily trained nurses administered basic care and comfort, ice packs and, it was said, gentle pinches to the nose.

I watched the news constantly; angel readings were put on hold. Scientists across the country set aside research projects to focus on the problem. Pfizer came up with a pill designed to control the bleeding, which was basically a common vasoconstrictive allergy drug in a new bottle. Coagulants were sometimes called upon, and the folks with really bad cases had to get their blood vessels cauterized, although bleeding rarely lasted more than a few minutes at a time. And—this was super weird, I watched a live show about it online—a handful of people reported severe bleeding, where blood actually flowed from the tear ducts. Once the Ebola virus was ruled out, they were questioned about their religious beliefs, in case they were displaying a variation on stigmata, bleeding like the suffering Christ statues in Bolivia. None of them claimed any affiliation.

And still I didn't bleed. I kept sitting through every red-rocked sunrise, trying to feel my chakras. I was checking my face thirty times an hour for blood.

I tuned into my podcast, too, as the thing spread, and somehow the podcast managed to get the attention of mainstream media. The idea went viral after the first FOX radio show. The Lunar Hoax website had twenty thousand hits in one hour. In one day, nearly half the world suddenly knew about the Spaceship Moon theory. The American space shuttle program, with a moon rocket at the ready, had just recently been shut down, but now astronauts were swiftly brought up to snuff for the voyage. We had to get back up there and see what was what.

This was when Warren called me.

"Wassup, girl?" He always put on an accent, just to make me laugh.

"Oh, you know. Living in paradise."

"You still okay down there?"

I didn't know if he meant the States or my womanly parts. "All good."

"Nothing's happening up here, so far. Canada's still clean. There's lots of talk about the bleeding, though," he said. "You . . . affected?"

"No. Not yet."

He was quiet. Then he said, "Come home, Lacy."

"I'm not done here."

"I need you up here."

His voice was making me cry. "What do you need?"

He laughed his velvet laugh and it felt like I was burning up. "What do you think?"

I was waiting it out. I wanted to see what side of things I was on. If I bled, aliens were trying to control me. If I didn't bleed, well, maybe I didn't need to. Maybe I was one of them. Maybe this was exactly why I'd been drawn to Sedona in the first place.

"Not yet," I told Warren. "I'm on the brink of a breakthrough. But thank you for calling, Warren of Canada." I'd been listening to too many call-in shows.

* * *

Just days before the scheduled launch of the Lunar Pilgrim shuttle, the noses of America stopped bleeding.

Oh, the odd child, nose-picker, or hockey player still got a garden-variety nosebleed, and every time it happened, people around the blood looked skyward, but it seemed that immediately after the wave of speculation about aliens being responsible had swept the globe, it was over. No more blood.

I'd been spared, or I'd been overlooked. I didn't know what to feel.

Despite the blood stopping, the Lunar Pilgrim went forth as planned, and the reports came back: still a moon, still four and a half billion years old, still orbiting Earth, showing only its one side because of synchronous rotation. My magnificent, rocky moon was back.

The Lunar Hoaxers were interviewed once more, and they just laughed. Aliens were crafty, they said. No doubt those astronauts were taken inside and made to believe what the aliens planted in their heads.

The podcast host asked, "What can be done?"

"If y'all see a spacecraft, run," they said.

It became a joke, with a *So You Think You Can Write Songs*

competition on TV, hosted by Ryan Seacrest, where contestants had to write a song using that lyric in the chorus: *If y'all see a spacecraft, run.* The winner would get to make a video in Hollywood, complete with green Martians and Drew Barrymore.

But then, one day in September, after I'd been in Sedona for three scorching months, a stronger gravitational pull began to affect people. To move took sweat-inducing amounts of effort, and no one knew where to point the finger because gravity was still a mystery, despite scientists claiming they were closer to measuring gravitons than ever before.

Extra gravity didn't impact me, either. What was wrong with me?

Warren phoned again. "Now will you come home, baby? I just heard that there's a place near Hudson Bay where gravity isn't as strong. We could go there. Try again."

Just a few hours' flight away, I had a man who wanted me, enlightened or not. I was alone in a foreign land and no closer to seeing angels or aliens. But then I received an email: a Groupon for an acre of moon surface. For $19.99 I could buy an official, notarized deed from the Lunar Embassy Corporation. A man named Dennis Hope owned the moon, after all, and he wasn't an alien, either, just a businessman from Nevada out to colonize a bit more of the solar system.

I was so lucky I'd acted as quickly as I did. He sold off all the acreage on the moon in a matter of days.

* * *

A few days later, my body began to feel lighter. Gravity's effects were lessening. I didn't need Hudson Bay. And I wasn't alone.

Many of those who were beginning to float knew that the only sensible thing was to take a lunar vacation, and we made our way to the launching site of the Lunar Pilgrim, at the Kennedy Space Centre in Florida, in hopes that it would take us all away.

In a hotel room in Dallas, I had to tie my legs and one wrist to the bed to get any sleep. While many people in the country were unable to get out of bed—as if the globe's core was pulling on every cell they had to keep them on Earth, as if Earth itself was worried that people would leave it behind—I was being freed. It was letting me go. No wonder I'd always felt out of place.

I had a shuttle to catch.

When I had everything set up in Florida, I called Warren to say goodbye. "I've got incredible news!"

"You're coming back?"

"Not exactly. But I've been chosen! I'm going to the moon."

He laughed. "Girl, are you finally trying peyote?"

"It's real, Warren. This is it. I've found my place in the universe."

"Lacy," he said, "I'm coming down to get you."

"I'm not in Sedona," I told him. "I'm already gone."

✳ ✳ ✳

As we glided away from the beautiful, magnetic, uninhabitable Earth, I looked back at the planet. What swirled above the blue marble, above the glassy green, were clouds of angels. Clouds of angels, in gowns of white, singing me home.

Adios

We used to exchange zucchinis for tomatoes, Fred Poole and I. At the house across the street from ours he used to garden early in the spring, before most people had finished their winter pruning. He liked to say hello in foreign languages as we walked past, when Simon was still a toddler enthralled by his own shadow. No matter the weather, Mr. Poole was out there, pruning or planting or propping something up.

Now Mrs. Poole is at the door. Her face is puffy, blotchy; she's been crying. Simon is suddenly beside me, asking if he can watch TV.

"Fred's gone," she says. "He's been taken by the Lord."

Taken? Oh, *that* taken. Oh, God. "Oh, Mrs. Poole," I say. "I'm so sorry."

"Over by the school," she says. "He got hit."

"Yes," I say to Simon, distracted. "Go ahead."

I'm sweating, shaking. I feel like throwing up. When I hear the TV come on, the music of a nature show that Simon loves, I stupidly ask Mrs. Poole, "By a car?" I imagine myself in her shoes, my husband, just like a young Mr. Poole, filled with beams of love for me, and then gone. My husband doesn't exist, and never did. But that fact doesn't matter: my brain conjures him up often enough that if I close my eyes, a whole scene—a whole life—unfolds.

"He never leaves the yard." Mrs. Poole's voice is quavering. "You ever seen him wandering around?"

"Um, once or twice." My words come out tiny and tight. "Out for a little walk."

Her eyes are welling up. "I was just getting the vegetables ready for dinner, and when I came out, he was gone. The policeman said it happens all the time, the wandering off, but Fred never did that kind of thing." She's still wearing her apron, embroidered with chickens.

Again, I stammer, "I'm so sorry."

Then, as if something has pushed her from behind, Mrs. Poole stands up taller. "Well," she says, wiping at her eyes with the cuff of her cardigan. "We shouldn't feel sorry, should we? God's got him. He's in the Lord's care now."

Simon is calling me to come and watch something.

"You go, now," Mrs. Poole says, opening her hands like she's Jesus showing his wounded hands, then pushing the air toward Simon. "God bless."

She makes her way slowly across the street, back to the empty house where now, with the Lord's help, she only has herself to take care of.

✳ ✳ ✳

Simon's eating from a giant box of Ritz crackers while glued to the show. The sight of my son makes me weepy.

"Look at the size of that, Mommy!"

The animal on the screen looks like a giant hamster, and it's rolling around in mud. I can't remember the name of the animal, but I know that I know; I studied mammals at university, in the days before making a mammal of my own.

"Wow," I say. "Pretty cool." What's its name? The name has something to do with Catholics down in South America—they were allowed to eat its meat during Lent because the animal used to be classified as a fish. Obviously it's not the right time for animal name recall. But what do I know about timing? "What's it called?"

"I dunno." Simon shrugs. "Wanna watch with me?"

"Maybe in a little while." That box of Ritz has me feeling guilty. I've got to cook up something decent for that boy. I need to make him eat better, foods that will feed his brain. They sent home a sheet from his school with those kinds of foods listed, but it's long gone into the recycling bin. All I remember is omega something-something. I grab my phone and Google "brain foods": the only ones on the list that he'll eat are walnuts, eggs as long as they're mixed into other ingredients, and blueberries. Guess it's muffin time.

The cookbook is from Mrs. Poole's church: all the ladies' favourite recipes, bound with a black plastic spiral. At the sight of its pale blue cover, I start to cry.

I saw Mr. Poole today and I did nothing.

It's all right, Jonathan, my made-up man, tells me, my head on his chest. *Our son is safe.* Like me, he gauges everything against Simon's safety. Jonathan is the guy who starts the high-fives, the one with the open, hug-ready arms. He's earned his wrinkles from sunshine, kindness, and wonder—the perpetual Boy Scout, collecting badges from a world he sees as harmonious and good. Simon has his love for the world, his grin.

I've helped kill a man. I'm looking right at him, my face broken and wet.

He stares back at me, then peeks through the archway to Simon, and I do the same. Simon's still watching TV. Crumbs litter the couch.

You didn't.

I might as well have done it myself. I let him get run over. I'm trembling.

You didn't know. He could've been okay.

He's dead. Fred Poole is dead.

* * *

Two years ago, Fred Poole got a gift from the Crown, the coronary vessels circling the heart like a tiara of thorns. A piece of the past had come back to haunt him, a package sent floating like the baby in the basket, Moses in the bulrushes, up to the Pharaoh's sister, arteries connecting to the Lord of all, the Almighty brain. How many religious metaphors does it take to give the picture?

The Pooles don't believe in medical intervention. Fred had a stroke. He didn't go to the hospital.

Today, I saw him, out walking. It was a beautiful day, and I just kept going. It was a timing error—I didn't have the time. He really did seem to be out for a walk, and only three blocks from his house, after all. I continued on to the schoolyard.

Another name for a stroke: cerebrovascular accident.

It wasn't an accident, Mrs. Poole would say. Nothing is accidental. She believed in strange blessings, that it was her duty to God to care for her husband; the stroke was a message to have faith, an opportunity for members of the congregation to work together. They believed they could heal him with prayer.

Does she know that the word *blessing* comes from the old German word *bletsian*, meaning blood? A souvenir from times when they performed regular sacrifices to God?

Following the stroke, Mr. Poole could only say three words. For no, he said, *Boy*. For yes, he said, *Boy oh boy*. When he didn't like something, he said, *Balls!* No one thinks to say that any more, but his wife still reddened, apologized, and mumbled into his ear, *Now, Fred*. She tried valiantly to make sure he liked everything, but she couldn't keep track. His frozen face said nothing at all, yet he could shuffle-walk when he needed to. His body was doing better than his brain.

After I ignored Fred today, I heard sirens coming closer while I waited for Simon. I smiled blandly at the other parents. It's nothing, I told myself. It isn't anyone I know. I found a piece of gum in my pocket and chewed the daylights out of it while I waited, doing what I had to do: pick up my son and go home. I said to myself that I didn't hear any screeching tires.

"Mom!" Simon called when he came running out of school. "Ambulance!"

He was fascinated by sirens, and before I was able to stop him, he was running down the sidewalk toward the blue car stopped in the middle of the street, the driver's door flung open. Simon didn't notice the man, half under the car, or recognize the plaid slipper by the curb. He was more interested in the flashing lights. My whole body weakened, lost feeling, until I realized what my son was about to see.

"Come on," I said, yanking him by the arm before he could get a better look. "It's just an ambulance. We're going home."

* * *

After the stroke it was months until I saw Mr. Poole outside. When Simon and I passed him, sitting in a reclining lawn chair, his garden overgrown and drab, I called out, "Buenos dias!" Fred looked confused and gripped the arm of the chair with his good hand. "Look!" Simon held up his toy for Fred to see. "I got a new yo-yo!" But Fred couldn't respond. He closed his eyes. "Adios," I said quietly and reached for Simon's shoulder as we walked away.

I thought of Fred's mind as a prison, trapping him with his three words. But some days, at home with the list of must-dos and Hot Wheels in every corner and work orders for more of my designer pillows piling up in my email inbox, no one coming home to help me clean it all up, Jonathan no support at all, I grew to envy him. Nothing to do but sit.

On other days, I felt angry with Fred, on his patch of grass, staring at anything that might come by. I might have hazarded the thought that he deserved it. Or else his wife did, all her bravado and clarity about the will of God. *Medical treatment is a necessity*, I wanted to yell, like getting enough protein, or sleep, whatever's required. Of course prayer is helpful. But not as therapy. Not as a substitute for an intravenous drip.

***

I'm at the counter, measuring the dry ingredients, when ghost-man Jonathan comes up behind me and says something in my ear about helping me to forget this terrible day.

I've got to tell her, I say.

He shakes his head. *It won't bring him back.*

But how can I face her every day?

You'll think of something, he says. *But first, come with me.*

As I'm walking with him to the bedroom, feeling my way with my eyelids firmly shut, the telephone rings.

"Phone!" Simon yells.

It rings again.

"Phone!"

Eyes open. Bye-bye, Jonathan.

After I say hello twice, I hear a shaky voice on the other end. "It's Annie Poole."

"Hi, Mrs. Poole." Is she telepathic? Listening in on my conversations?

"I've slipped," she says. "I think my ankle might be broken."

Maybe Mrs. Poole just wants me to show that I'm still a good person, that I can make choices that would make her God happy. Otherwise, why not call 9-1-1? Oh, right. No medical intervention. No X-ray, plaster cast, or padded crutch for her. She's not trying to give me anything; I'm just handy.

Or maybe she knows I saw him today. She's giving me a chance to make it up, or confess. She knows how much better it feels to offer up your mistakes to the Lord for pardon, and she wants me to feel this, too. She wants to give me this, forgiveness like birds flying out of my chest, a lightness I haven't felt since my last confession at least ten years ago.

"I'll be right there," I tell her.

I look in on Simon. "Don't move. I have to go across the street." He's zoned into the show; he doesn't even know I'm talking.

Suddenly, I remember the name of the animal he's watching. Capybara. It tastes like pork. Maybe Simon would eat something weird like this, the largest rodent-mammal in the world, instead of his beloved white flour and sugar.

My mind holds on to so many things it doesn't need. No wonder my head feels as full as it does. The curse of my species, to have thoughts; the blessing, too.

Despite the circumstances, a rush of hope rises in me. "It's a capybara," I yell to Simon. "Capybara!"

"Okay," he calls back. "Bye."

Jonathan, I say, quietly. *Please keep him safe.* How's he going to like sharing couch space with Mrs. Poole, once I get her over here? Will he say, *Boy oh boy*, or *Boy*? More likely, *Balls*.

Jonathan doesn't answer. He can't hear me over the television.

* * *

Mrs. Poole is lying on her kitchen floor, a broken glass and a puddle of water beside her on the tiles. "You're an answer to a prayer," Mrs. Poole says. She's pale and shaking, but she smiles weakly at me. "You're a gift from God."

Flip

Monday morning. Claudia can see puffiness beneath Rodger's steel eyes, but his smile is big enough to show his upper gums and his good oral hygiene. His graphite hair is spiked up at intentional angles; when she uses a pencil today she will think of him. But when does she use a pencil? Her hands are curled into paws from keyboard use, her spine is a wilting stem. The library used to supply little pencils for the slips of paper to help people find their books, but they kept getting stolen. Now there are leashed pens, but rarely does she see anyone write anything down. Most store information in their phones, these people who have never looked in the drawer of a card catalogue, unless it's to buy one at a retro/hipster/upcycling boutique downtown. Do they even know who Melvil Dewey was? Honestly, the books seem to be props half the time. Everyone Googles. Only the elderly and the die-hards who hate screen views come into the library for books. The homeless outnumber the studious, two to one on rainy days, the smell of paper and binding is becoming replaced by urine, sour socks, and liniment, and her poor books languish on the shelves, filed in perfect Dewey Decimal order.

"Claudia," Rodger says in that singsong way, standing in front of Claudia's station at the information desk. "How was your weekend?"

He should know. He was there, at least at the beginning of it. On Friday night in the bustling retirement haven of Oak Bay Village, deep within the gentle folds of the city of Victoria, Rodger had been walking down the avenue toward her when she'd bolted. The stores were already tinselled up like tarts for the Christmas season, but she'd just been innocently picking up a decent loaf of bread from the Italian bakery when she saw him coming. She looked around for the nearest escape route and had to choose between Serious Coffee and an art gallery, and because he was wearing a puffy coat and talking on a cellphone, she chose art.

Wrong choice. Rodger came in and found her at the back of the long room, where she was rummaging in her purse for a tissue.

"Hey, Claudia," he said. "You like the show?"

She hadn't looked at the art until he asked.

Everything was penises. The whole gallery was plugged with cocks, and most of them were up and ready, sculptures and paintings alike. One even had a handlebar moustache.

Her face bruised with blood, she nodded, then made a run for the door.

Now Claudia wants to give him more glamorous weekend details, but aside from working on her self-love according to the latest blog she's following, which has instructed her to do what she would do if a mate were in her life—cook a whole chicken with herbs and spices! Wear matching bra and panties! Brush hair and teeth once more each day!—her list includes eating two family-sized bags of barbecue chips, watching three bad movies, petting Ruffles, her mangy cat, and watching, for hours, a brown wren playing with its reflection in the broken mirror stored on her balcony.

Weekend. Same old, same old, aside from Cockland. He doesn't need to know.

"Pretty good," she says to Rodger. "How about you?"

"Bit of this, bit of that," he says, taking a bookmark out of the inviting display in front of her computer and turning it to face the right way. "Trying to decide on a vacay spot for January. You ever been to Aruba?"

"No." Aruba. It sounds like an old car's horn when she repeats it in her head.

"What about Cuba?"

"No." She's never been anywhere. Afraid of flying, along with a hundred other worries.

"Those are my top two picks," he tells her.

"Tough choice," she says. Why is he doing this? Can he not tell that she is the wrong person to ask about tropical vacations? She's a gong show, the way she folds into herself like one of those plastic toys you push on the bottom to make move—only she's not cute. She knows she needs help in coming out of herself, in making herself a part of the world, but she just can't do it. What would any other girl do when faced with a gallery of penises and a male colleague who likes to look her straight in the eye? Stick around and pick favourites? Analyze the finer points of penile art, remark on how she preferred the stone renditions to the canvas? She can barely get undressed in front of her own mirror; she rushes away like that wren, only to return to the same old bird. Nothing else to do but run.

Rodger has more questions. "Where would you go, Claudia? Like, if I handed you a ticket and said, Come with me, where would your heart prefer?"

Her heart? Her heart feels like a bag of puppies. When she doesn't answer because she has been rendered mute by this mere idea, he holds his hand open and looks straight into her eyes again.

"Got a coin?" he asks. "We'll flip."

He must be fooling. Flip a coin, choose a vacation spot? It's like those multiple-ending books she hated as a kid. She wants a book to begin, continue, and end—no flexibility, no decisions to make. A book offers answers, not a bunch of options.

She hands Rodger a loonie from her top drawer. Her Glossette raisins money.

"No," he says, hands up in protest. "You do the honours."

She has never flipped a coin. What does this madman see when he looks at her? Now he must see her tomato face, her tremoring hands, her open mouth. *Close your mouth, Claudia. Look alive!*

"Heads is Cuba, Claudia, tails is Aruba," he says. "Hey, that sounds like a song!"

She throws the coin into the air. It rises about two inches, then falls into her waiting hand.

"Oh, Claudia," he says. "Give it more of a chance to make up its mind, girl."

"Higher?" she asks.

"Higher! Make it work for you." He winks at her; she reddens. Rodger says her name more often than anyone else she's ever known. Some days he comes over to her desk and says it three times in a row: *Claudia, Claudia, Claudia.* He's seen her crimson face, her sputtering shoulders as she gets pulled forward and back by fear, when all she wants to do is break into a sprint and lock herself in the bathrooms down by the kids' books, even though she would have to run up the ramp—impossible to do without sounding like a stampeding gorilla. But still he says it, over and over.

She tosses the loonie higher. It flips several times, like a good coin should. When she catches it, it feels a little cooler than when she let it go. Her heart is racing, but what for? It's not for her that she's doing this. She's simply catering to a whim of a co-worker, who's so bored he's come to hang around the likes of her for diversion.

"Heads," she says and holds it out for Rodger to see.

"Cuba!" he cries, then grins as library patrons turn to stare. He lowers his voice. "Well, all right then. Cigar orders are being taken."

His smile makes Claudia plunk back down into her office chair.

"You think you can get two weeks?" Rodger asks her.

Error! Error! Error! flashes before her eyes. Malfunction in the universe's mainframe. He was serious when he asked her to go. No. It can't be.

He was serious?

∗ ∗ ∗

After her eventful work day, Claudia curls into her one big chair with a glass of Merlot and a sleeve of digestive cookies and opens her atlas to search for Rodger's islands.

Cuba is easy, but she looks around for at least five minutes before she locates Aruba, near the phallic north end of Columbia. Won't Rodger have a lovely time of it on either island, surrounded by all that warm water!

Oh, he's such a big flirt! Does he know how that could really mess with a girl? Not her, but another, more gullible one, who'd consider taking a trip with a relative stranger. She remembers his face in the art gallery: comfortable with all those penises around him. Well, that's to be expected, since he has one. Would she have been as calm in a room full of vulvas? Not a chance.

It's not like she doesn't think of them, penises. But when she does, it's a meagre selection she can draw from. Her love life has been rather limited. *You don't say, Claudia! Three penises in total!* She doesn't think of the one she first allowed inside her, at university—a poli-sci student she'd been pushed into meeting by her roommate; it had happened in a walk-in closet and was over before she could feel anything but the pain. Clark's doesn't really come to mind, either, her one-and-only real boyfriend from three years ago, a relationship that lasted just half a year. It's Runt's she returns to as needed. Her first impression of the beast.

In high school she was shy, too, but in more of a normal sense than she is now, the way most awkward girls with no cleavage/dimples/ money/slippery morals are. Her crushes had mostly involved the boys' volleyball team—a generic love of sandy blond and tall and blue, the garden variety where she'd come from in the Okanagan. She wasn't shooting for the genetic moon. But she never thought chances, never really picked one out and said, *Him.* It was like trying to pick the right golden Lab puppy. How could she choose?

One day, though, a miracle happened: a boy started looking her way. He was the runt of the litter, the boy on the bench at most games unless the flu had the others down. His glances turned from general to specific, from sporadic to regular, and Claudia stopped sleeping. She couldn't eat; she wrote furiously in her poor pink diary; she forgot to do her homework, until one day after the game, they were in the hallway together, and he motioned for her to follow him into the supply room. Alone at last.

Runt took her hand and put it where he wanted it. She held on and the penis was like a living branch in her grip, as if she could feel the earth's bubbling core directly through it. The skin was as soft as bunny ears, and she moved her hand lightly over it—a newborn animal. It wasn't long before her delicate scalp was being pushed on the spot where adults liked to pat her on the head, only this hand had force behind it; this hand was on a mission. What did she know about anything below the belt other than to stay away? He pushed her head down and she was face to face for the first time with a cocky cock, wanting her, only her, and somehow she got her mouth involved and with no skill at all aside from not using teeth—she'd heard that once, somewhere—she was dealing with Runt's burning juices, his half-babies dead in her throat. The sound he made was baby animal, too, and when she glanced up at him there was a passing cloud of love on his face. Then, a ten-second trip from bliss to watching his backside walk away from her, a mumbled thanks to Claudia in her praying position on the floor. She tried to stand. Her thighs had turned to sandbags, her feet to stone. All she wanted was a Halls mentholyptus and to magically fly home to bed. And perhaps, one day, to do that again.

Rodger must be messing with her. She's not used to this kind of attention, standing out as anything more than the roundish library lady pointing people in the right direction, helping them find mis-shelved books and the bathrooms. God, he might be pulling a *Carrie* stunt, befriending the loser as a kind of goodwill joke like they did in that horrible Stephen King movie.

How can she even think of going on a holiday? She doesn't even own a bathing suit!

✳ ✳ ✳

At lunch on Tuesday Claudia pulls out her chicken sandwich, still feeling the love from the bird she cooked on the weekend.

"Looks good," Helen says, but she may not mean it. She has sushi again. Claudia's seen her eat teaspoons of wasabi, watched as her face blushed from the heat but nothing—not a peep!—came from her mouth. Helen is strong and supple. She is somebody's yoga pet.

"Thanks," Claudia says. "I finally got busy and did some cooking."

Helen laughs her sharp laugh. "Looks like Rodger wants you to get a little busy, too."

Face burns, throat shuts, stomach rises. Claudia looks down at her fine-looking sandwich and tries to say, No, don't be ridiculous, who, me, you must be joking, but what comes out is this: "He asked me to go to Cuba with him."

"Cuba!" Helen shrieks. "That's wild, girl!"

Why are they both calling her girl lately? She's younger than Rodger, but she's no girl. Her neck feels rusted into place, her eye-balls stuck in the down position, but she forces herself to look at Helen. She's got to check for a smirk. Complicity. But Helen's just flashing her usual white gleam.

"Have you said yes?" she asks.

Claudia shakes her head. "I've got a cat."

As if that's the only reason she's holding back. *As if he actually meant it, girl!*

Truth is, sun makes Claudia break out in a rash and wince because of her light blue eyes. Her kind of joy is the year's first snowfall, when all the kids rush to the classroom windows. She can smell when snow is coming, and when it starts tumbling down so thick it's impossible to see through, her elation feels holy. That kind of snow rarely happens in this coastal city, so it's even more divine when it does. Why would she even want to go to Cuba?

It would be hot and sunny and she would puff up like a stung lip. If Rodger touched her, she would cry.

∗ ∗ ∗

It is that possibility—the touching—that leads to her knocking lightly on the head librarian's door after lunch on Wednesday. *What have you asked for, ever? Nothing! And what have they given you? Nothing!*

Her brain chants this protest song alongside the dualing taunts of *Stu-pid, Stu-pid* and *Red Rover, Red Rover, we call Loser over,* and yet somehow, after she asks for a couple of weeks off, she sees a nod and hears a yes and it's done. Claudia's sure her boss thinks she's a complete dud, so of course she wants her to do something for once in her life. Years ago, a rumour circulated about her boss and Rodger having an affair, so Claudia doesn't bring up his name. She doesn't need to. Nothing is set—she's just booked time off, no plans made. The snow will be decent in the BC interior then, if nothing else pans out. She's good to go!

A few minutes later, sadness settles in. Why bother with a vacation? It's senseless, really: the same shit waiting for you when you return, plus a whole whack of emails to slog through. Desire of any kind: is that sensible, either? Is it sensible to want anything, beyond what keeps the flesh alive and mobile? No. Where is the sense in taking a two-week holiday with a man she's never even invited over for dinner? What's going to come of it other than a bad burn?

* * *

Thursday morning. She and Ruffles sit by her patio door and watch the bird at the mirror again. It was Clark's mirror, something he tried to hang where Claudia's painting of mountains now hangs once more, but after only a week, it came crashing down, cracking all along the bottom. She can't bear to throw it away: what else does that bird have to play with? The bird hops away or flies a few feet straight up, then returns to its reflection, as if it's giving the mirror bird a chance to either escape or follow. It doesn't work. Ignoring it doesn't, either. Peck, peck. Kisses or combat? It's impossible to tell.

She can't remember what she and Clark did as a couple during their six-month relationship. He worked out or played soccer daily; she didn't. He worked evenings at a pub; she worked days. On weekends they shopped for groceries and played along with *Family Feud* reruns on TV. Once they went hiking together at the lake, and a pit-bull puppy chased her. Sex had been regimented to not coincide with soccer matches or his sleep needs, which didn't often match up with her desire or non-period days, so it was sporadic at best. When they did do it, he liked her to feel his ass, to hold on, as if he were waiting for compliments about its tone. He never asked her what she wanted. *And what was that, Claudia?* An orgasm would've been nice, if it wasn't too much to ask for. And yet, it was. She never asked, it never happened, and one day, in a text, he told her he was moving to Alberta for oil sands work. It was the best place for him and his overdeveloped lats.

What Claudia has seen from Rodger is a hundred times better than any of this; he looks like the kind of guy who walks into a restaurant and secretly pays for everyone's lunch. Magnaminous. Still, she is uncertain about taking a trip with the man. What sense does it all make?

Back to sense again. Many people would say that a cat is senseless and she has one of those—an especially senseless one that watches life from behind this patio window, a cat that ignores her more than not. And yet, she loves Ruffles. Claudia has read about how love can change a person, even on a cellular level. Besides the moony eyes, the mushy brain, a connection with another human can actually make you healthier. It can give you a longer life. She wonders if loving a cat can do the same.

She hasn't even told Rodger she can go yet. Could he grant her the wish she's had for years, to be able to set her head down on a man's belly and have it be safe, a cuddle, a place to rest? *Claudia, come on. Is that all you want?* Along with climaxing, that is. Friendship and sex, both from the same person, right beside her. Would Rodger's magnaminity offer her this, too?

*** ***

Thursday afternoon. Claudia has been looking at the mouths of teenagers when they come into the library today. Gum is not her worry: she's looking for a sign that they've done it, or would do it. She looks at colours of lip gloss, shininess, has read that there are codes for what's going down—or who. Oral fixation begins at the nipple, of course, but are there girls out there who want a penis in their mouths? All those mouths once wiped by mothers, smooched by relatives who wanted a kiss before anyone could leave, those mouths eating birthday cake and sucking on licorice whips and Tootsie Pops and Mr. Freezies, one big practice for the real thing. All-day suckers. Icicles taken straight from the roof. Old-fashioned peppermint sticks. If she looks at it this way, girls practise their whole lives.

When Rodger makes his mid-afternoon rounds, checking in with his information desk girls, she dares to meet his gaze.

"Hola, señorita," he says. He does a little dance with his hips. "You ready to rumba?"

It's ridiculous, it's mad, they only know each other in the coffee sense, that is, she likes lattes with extra sugar, he likes Africanos, and her face is burning again, but before she can stop herself, she says yes. "Si, señor." Her vocal cords are doing double dutch with her terrible Spanish so it comes out as a gargle. Last chance to say something else. To pretend she was trying to say sorry, or so sad, to spare herself. *Spit it out, woman!* She tries again, in English. "Yes," she says. "Let's book it."

He puts up his hand for a high-five. "Well, all righty then!" He's smiling as though he's actually going to go through with it. He wasn't pulling her leg. He wants her to go.

She raises her hand. She lets him touch it. First touch. A sealed deal.

Before she leaves for home, she checks out a Lonely Planet Cuba and a book about strategies for flying without fear. Somehow she makes it onto the right bus and into her apartment, but it is not until she's back in her armchair pushing Ruffles off her open atlas that she realizes what she's done, where she's going. She traces the route their flight will most likely take—a sideways swipe across the continent to Florida, then just a bit further to that long and curvy island about to enter the Gulf of Mexico.

She wants to see a cloud forest. Take photos of animals she can't pronounce the names of. Drink something that might make her able to dance.

* * *

Then, after a week of eating lunch together in various cafés in town, getting to know each other better, looking in the guidebook for things to do and see, Rodger gives her some bad news: his elderly mother has passed away.

He takes a leave of absence from the library, is out of town for a month, including over Christmas, to tidy up the estate and to find, unsuccessfully, a new home for his ma's big old tabby, who now belongs to him.

They have a rocking time of it, though, via email. Claudia is at her ultra-best on screen, flirty as the scent of waffle cones, intelligent and witty and deep. Rodger is still a charmer, but he comes off as less pushy via words, although she does miss the sight of his grey eyes, his quick grin. And, even better, now he has a cat!

It hurts when she has to log off to go to sleep or work. She misses the sound of his voice, saying her name. *Red Rover, Red Rover, we call Claudia over!*

* * *

During Rodger's time away, she hears a woman tell her friend a story on the bus home from work one day. A boy was born, second son in the family, and given the name John. As soon as he could form sentences, he pointed to himself and said, Me Evan. No, his mother kept saying. You're John. No, Evan. No, John. It went on and on, the mother completely beside herself because her father had died years before John was born, and his name had been Evan. When the boy got older he was able to explain it: yes, he was Evan, his grandfather, living again. The mother believed him; she had to. He was so much like her father in mood and temperament that she couldn't doubt him. When he was able, he legally changed his name to Evan and has been Evan ever since.

Claudia feels like another person has entered her body. *Who are you, girl? Has someone come back from the dead to inhabit you?* She can't come up with anyone; she is just Claudia, the woman who fled from a man and a room full of penises, yet somehow is at the start of a new relationship with the same man. Isn't she the same woman? Or is there a new girl in residence within? Or is it just that a part of her, seemingly dead or missing, is being brought back to life, a little resurrection? There all the time, in fact: in her the whole time—she's just needed some help in bringing her out. Whenever Rodger says her name, it feels like he's pulling her out of the deep well of herself. *Claudia.* One more yank toward the top. *Claudia.* Even closer to the light.

✳ ✳ ✳

When they see each other the first day they're back at work together, her eyes are filled with needles of excitement, pointing only at Rodger. He leans over and whispers that the trip is booked, and her whole body turns to goosebumps. She turns her face to check his expression and his lips are there, below his dead-serious eyes. She swipes her own lips across them, and zap! They give each other an electric shock.

The universe's mainframe has been reprogrammed.

She's going to Cuba.

✳ ✳ ✳

Their flight departs in a few days. She has bought herself a colourful beach towel, a tankini, and a floppy white hat; she has packed flouncy dresses and even a sheer nightgown, should the occasion arise to need one. They have worked out all the details: they each have a cat sitter, and their workmates will hold down the fort while they slip into the salty sea.

The night before they leave, Claudia cannot sleep. Or if she does, it is only to dream out her anxiety, mainly about being all alone and lost in a foreign country. She tries to focus on what has happened between her and Rodger, which doesn't take long: that zap of a first kiss at the library, a kiss in the car when he dropped her off one night. A hug that felt like a whole season had come and gone when he finally let her go. Still, it is enough to keep her awake, worried that she is in over her head. She's a librarian. She's used to loving books, not people! She looks around and loves them all, just waiting on their shelves to be chosen.

And what do you wish for them, Claudia? To be touched, taken home, opened.

Three hours until morning, until the airport shuttle honks its arrival to take her away.

Only one room booked.

* * *

On the airplane they watch their own movies and Claudia falls asleep against Rodger's shoulder, behaviour that has her blinking with embarrassment when she sees drool on his shirt. He doesn't seem to mind. They land in Cuba and both of them are sweating even before they leave the plane, which makes her feel better about Rodger than she did before, if that is possible. He sweats in heat, too. He's real!

Voilà! No, *Aquí!* Here it is. Cuba.

Sweat rolls off their faces as they roll their suitcases away from the carousel and out into the wham of fragrant warmth.

Rodger takes her slippery hand in his slippery hand and they stare out the taxi windows. What she sees as they cruise the streets of Havana on their way to the hotel is nothing like what she's imagined, even though her guidebooks have plenty of photos.

A child carrying a baby pig. Men wearing straw hats, playing stand-up bass and drums. Women and girls who move their hips in ways she's never seen, just walking down the street. Old people in doorways, watching old cars pass. Women with gigantic cigars in their mouths, looking like they're enjoying themselves immensely.

Rodger points. "Interested in one of those?"

Claudia doesn't need to think about it. "Yes," she says.

Oh, God, yes.

Tropical Dreams

Everyone told us the chances of seeing a crocodile were minimal. They're nocturnal. Shy. Not waiting to pose for us. And yet there we were, at the garbage dump on the small island of Caye Caulker, diseases swirling in the filth beneath our flip-flops, because a croc was supposed to be in residence there.

This was Day One of our tropical vacation in Belize. Yay, us.

Allan led the hunt in the searing afternoon heat. Our winter-weary skin was fresh meat for the equatorial sun; we'd arrived that morning via water taxi after flying into Belize City. We looked like beige Barbie dolls. We were going to fry, and I was okay with that.

On a small hill he spotted the woman who lived on-site, we'd been told, tidying up the junk around the junk that was her world. "We hear there's a croc or two here," Allan called.

She shook her head above a spine with a serious curve and told us not to bother. "All de kids scare 'em away," she told us. "With rocks." She sounded upset.

Smart kids. Then I looked at my husband, Fraser, and Allan, his friend from university, the thrill of the hunt in their eyes—they looked like little kids.

The woman closed the door of her plywood shack.

"Well, that blows," Allan said, hands on hips.

"Total letdown," Fraser said. I heard the irony in his voice, but I'm not sure Allan did.

Then we heard a shriek. Allan's girlfriend, Billy, younger than the rest of us by at least ten years, had her hands over her mouth—a mistake, putting your fingers anywhere near your mouth in a garbage dump—and was pointing to a puddle.

Allan rushed over. "You see one?"

"Oh, my God, it's terrible," she said.

She'd found a drowned kitten.

"Ah, shit," Allan said. "I thought we'd hit the jackpot."

* * *

Fraser and I were fading at home in Vancouver, the way goldfish lose their colour when they're in a dark room. Neither of us had taken a southern vacation before: Fraser was miserly, and I was too afraid of disease, after seeing awful things in my training as a care aid—and then at work, at the group home—that might have been prevented by basic hygiene. But we needed vitamin D, badly, and to breathe in air that wasn't half-water.

According to the websites, Belize was cheap, had decent snorkelling, and lacked Starbucks. Fraser invited Allan and Billy. The four of us spent fall and winter in our respective cities, plotting flights and vaccinations and assortments of snacks and small pharmaceuticals, texting each other often. Fraser was a substitute teacher, French immersion, at a different school almost every day. Allan was some kind of faux-finisher, making murals of rustic scenes for the urbanites of Calgary. Billy was a nursing student, her training almost complete. We all wanted out of our cages; we all wanted some R & R.

* * *

After the garbage dump excursion, Billy and I rinsed our legs in the turquoise ocean and coated them in hand sanitizer as an extra protection from parasites. Then, we walked to the other end of the village, to take a dip in the local swimming hole, the Hurricane Iris–ruined pier, because the guide book I'd brought said the swimming was better.

The water was too warm, like swimming in someone's mouth. And yet it felt so good to be nearly naked, up to our necks in water and with a sky that wouldn't pour sheets of cold, grey rain down on us. Fraser found a lid from a plastic ice cream tub on the beach and tossed it like a Frisbee. I caught it and sent it flying back.

Billy cried, "Oh, I'm terrible at this," when it was her turn to throw. The lid landed about two feet in front of her.

Fraser, the hero, swam over, rescued the lid, and aimed it at me. "It just takes practice."

"Oh, you're so good," Billy called. "Allan, did you see that?"

Allan was not into the game. He was lying on the cement pier, a meaty forearm strapped over his eyes.

I threw the lid to Billy. "Sue, you too!" She giggled. "A poet and I don't know it." When she tossed the lid, her perfect little boobies bounced like tiny porpoises. I noticed Fraser trying not to look. Her belly ring caught the light when she jumped above the surface. Ahhh. There was sunlight! There was hope!

* * *

Over dinner at a beachside restaurant, Fraser and Allan looked like tired surfers. Billy's blond cap of hair was sticking up stylishly from the salt water, while my bottle-black mane hung thick with sand and knots. Hot wind blew off the water. Billy had put her peach T-shirt back on over her swimsuit, but I could hear her nipples saying, Hey, old lady, you think your husband can keep away for long? I don't remember what we ate—the food in Belize was categorically unmemorable. I just remember Billy's little voice, her ginger-ale giggle, my husband's responding laughter, and Allan's one-word grunts. I remember that peach T-shirt.

Fraser and I had been married for three years. We liked being married. We liked the strange thrill it gave us to say "husband and wife" because in certain circles it felt like we'd done something wrong. We both were products of broken marriages, and to come out the other side and still go willingly into the gold band and double-named cheques said something about us, we thought. Our parents' infidelities and neuroses wouldn't enter the utopia of our marriage.

Our marriage: utopian? Fraser was looking at those Billy boobs. Of course he was.

* * *

That night, the sky proved me wrong. The rain that fell was over-achiever rain. A torrential, outlandish amount of rain. We had to run from the restaurant to our hotel, and when we arrived, the staff was playing cards by candlelight in the lobby. We darted around buckets and towels on the tile stairs and made it to our room, where water was leaking in from under the balcony door.

We staunched the flow with every towel in the room. Fraser wanted to sit on our balcony's plastic chairs and watch the rain.

"You're serious? We came all this way to get out of the rain and you want to watch it here?"

"Nothing like this happens at home. No rain with this kind of drama."

True. No power except the weather. Being without electricity wasn't so bad—we were on holiday, out of the dismal winter, ready to relax. And yet, I wasn't relaxed.

"I wonder if Allan's room is flooding, too." Fraser scratched a bite on his ankle. Billy and Allan had left the restaurant before us so she could medicate a migraine brought on from the change in baro-metric pressure. They'd fought over the number of drinks Allan was consuming, too. She'd actually put her hand over his wineglass when the waiter tried to fill it.

"What's wrong?" Fraser asked me. "You've been quiet all night."

"I'm fine. Just thinking." What was I thinking? About Fraser's eyes on Billy's body. Not about Fraser's eyes.

"We're on vacation. You're not supposed to think."

"It's finally cooler," I said. "It's the first time I've been *able* to think."

Five minutes later we heard Billy and Allan, fighting. Then, a minute later, a switch to moaning. The fight as foreplay.

"I thought she had a migraine."

He shrugged.

I lowered my voice to a whisper. "It sounds like they're on the flipping balcony."

Fraser laughed. "That's just like Allan. Never one to hide his feelings."

"I'm going in." My shorts were wet and tight around my ass. I lifted out of the low chair with a sexy squelch.

Fraser grabbed my arm as I stood up. "Can I come?"

"I thought you wanted to listen . . . to the storm."

"I've heard enough."

It got us both going, hearing them. He initiated the kisses, and I didn't stop him. As Fraser roamed my body, I told myself that beauty was beauty; it didn't need to be categorized further. My thoughts were my own territory. I could do anything in my tropical dreams.

* * *

The next day we took a snorkelling trip to the coral reef that runs the length of the whole country. Fraser and Allan were delighted to touch nurse sharks and manta rays. The two men were in their glory, sunburned faces popping up every few minutes to exclaim how totally amazing it all was. The sharks only suck on your skin, the tour guide assured us as he threw cat food into the water.

No worries. Gentle animals. No crocs out here. The fish were spectacular—neon and bright and flashing between us through the coral brains and branches that hadn't been destroyed by hurricanes.

The tour concluded with a one-hour stop on Ambergris Caye, the bigger island to the north. The guide found a lunch place on the beach, and after some mediocre fish burgers and really loud reggae, the four of us sought some shade to wait for the boat to leave. We were jet-lagged and sun-weary by then, and the only shade was from the shadows of the bright buildings or beneath gigantic coconut palms. I'd read the guidebook: not a wise place to sit. Still, Allan insisted.

"What are the chances? The odds are pretty slim."

The rest of us floated in the water. I was nearly asleep when Allan shouted, interrupting our reverie. "What the fuck? Billy, come help me!"

He was sitting up, rubbing his shoulder, glaring at us as we waded back to shore through the tepid waves, fast as we could.

"There's the coco loco," Billy said when we reached Allan. She pointed at the green coconut the size of a Nerf football. "Or should I say 'smart coconut'? It must've heard you."

Allan held one palm over the hurt shoulder. "You think it's funny, a broken bone?" He wasn't smiling.

"Oh, Allan," Billy said. "You're all right."

"This is my painting arm," he said. "If I don't paint, you suffer."

Billy looked as though she'd been slapped in the face. We knew he'd been paying her way through university, paying for everything so she didn't need to work while studying. They'd met when she was sixteen, fresh out of a bad boyfriend scenario, and he'd footed the bill from then on. He'd virtually raised her.

Fraser looked around. "There's our guide, heading back to the boat. Maybe he's got some ice in the drinks cooler for your arm."

"I'm all right," Allan said, on his back again on his towel. "Billy, go buy me a beer for the pain."

She rose and started toward the restaurant. She turned and gave me a helpless look. I caught up with her. "Can I borrow a few bucks? It's better if I don't ask Mr. Happy for cash right now."

I handed her an American twenty. "Get one for each of us."

* * *

The next afternoon, we took the water taxi back to Belize City to catch a bus going south. We were on our way to Placencia, a small town on the southern coast, a place, according to the book, with the best beaches in Belize and the best gelato in the world.

The water taxi station was a bus station, too. While we waited for our bus, a man wove in and out of the crowd, saying, "Tsewi!" He carried a box full of bottles. Billy bought one—a seaweed drink that came in reused water bottles—and then, I couldn't believe it, she drank it.

"Not bad," she said. "Sue, give it a try."

"No way. I only have so much Imodium with me."

Billy made Allan take her picture with a local girl in tiny braids, snot running into her smile. The girl's mother, dancing around to call attention to herself and disappearing for long minutes at a time, was possibly a prostitute. Then, although touching a strange animal was so careless, especially for a nursing student, Billy cuddled with a coati. The owner of this weird raccoon/ anteater mash-up claimed he was a vet and that he could ship one to her for only fifty dollars. She wanted to take one right there and then. She was so naive, I envied her; I'd never been that kind of innocent.

We made it onto our bus without any tropical animals, and despite the heat and the Bob Marley blasting, Allan fell asleep. I was halfway through a novel, Fraser put earphones in and played a video game on his phone, Billy, in the seat in front of me, opened her textbook and flipped through the pages.

"Do you miss work yet?" She'd turned around and rested her baby-fresh chin on the back of her seat, like a puppy would. The Belizeans around us stared at her.

Which part might I miss? The holding of the piss bottle or the sponge bathing? The washing of other peoples' dishes or the meticulous records I had to keep to ensure the group home was funded for another year? "Not yet," I told her. "You miss school?"

"God, no," she said. "We're doing practical work now." She kneeled to face me fully. "You know, bodies are pretty gross, Sue."

I snorted. "Really."

Her lips puckered. "I'm not sure if I can go through with it."

"With what?"

"This program. All those sick people, looking at me, needing me." She glanced at Allan, snoring beside her. "Allan thinks I should become a flight attendant."

God. From one blond caregiving stereotype to another. "That's a bit extreme," I said.

She shook her head. "I'm considering it. I've had a lot of waitressing experience, and I'm a good flyer—"

"But what do *you* want?"

She took a huge breath and let out an enormous sigh. "I want to stay here and forget about everything!"

Allan raised his groggy head. "Keep it down, will you?"

Bob Marley's song "Sun Is Shining" came on then. Billy turned around to face the front of the bus again and sang along. I watched her browned shoulders dance. Fraser pulled his headphones out. "What'd I miss?"

✳ ✳ ✳

After hours of school bus–style travel along marginal roads through small villages and groves of dusty orange trees, after switching buses in Belmopan and again in Dangriga, after too much reggae and too many granola bars, we made it to Placencia. We checked into our shared cottage on the beach, then dropped everything to take a swim. The orange starfish looked like cartoons, fat beauties that didn't resist us picking them up like the ones back home. The beach was coarse sand—not the typical perfect sand as I'd imagined, but the water was clear and clean and warm and calm. We all washed the bus trip away in the briny blue.

Billy swam away from the rest of us. After a minute I checked on her. She was floating on her back, no bathing suit top in sight.

Fraser and Allan were already on the beach. I removed my top and wrapped it around my wrist. Booby sway, water tongues, I took a deep breath and floated face down. It felt free and right for about five seconds, until I had a thought. Nipples might look like bait to a passing fish. I turned over onto my back. Billy might've looked over; I don't know.

When we emerged, tops back on, the guys were talking about sports. Sports! Fraser never watched sports, as far as I knew, and yet he was full-on into having opinions about teams and players, arguing about who'd win the Stanley Cup. Billy and I lay down and absorbed some rays until a young girl came over and offered us a handbill for a Happy Hour, two for one at the nearest bar-restaurant.

We raced back to the cottage, dried off, and changed quickly so we'd get a table. Over a dinner of chicken fingers and fries, I watched the three of them proceed to get plastered. I was on the wagon because I couldn't stand the taste of dark rum. We were in Rumville, and rum was all they served.

Billy leaned over and told me she thought I was exotic-looking. "You and Fraser make a beautiful couple."

Sweet little slosh-face. "Thanks."

After dinner, Fraser and Allan looked through the guidebook for things to do in the area. They listed choices aloud: whale shark tours, game fish expeditions, lagoon kayaking.

"All I really want to do is lie down and bake," I said.

Billy agreed with me. The sun was making her hair turn white, like Swedish kids' hair. She was becoming younger before my eyes. Just a girl with excellent boobies. Right then, they were trying their best to remain inside a green halter dress, without much luck.

The guys protested our laziness but agreed to give us the night to make a decision. "We can't just lie around like bums."

"Says who?" I asked Fraser.

He pointed at Allan, who laughed. "Can we at least agree on checking out the gelato after dinner?"

We agreed.

"But first, one more drink for everyone."

"Hold the rum," I said to our waiter, who wanted to pollute my Coke.

Then a teenaged boy stopped at our table with two black and white puppies. "Hey, mon, you wantin' a puppy? Take one home wit' you. Good price."

Billy went off. "Oh, look, Allan, we have to take them! They're so darling!"

Allan's face was red from booze and sun. "They're pretty damn cute," he said.

"We could adopt them, right? People do it all the time."

Fraser shook his head. "It's a hassle. You don't want to bother."

Billy looked at the boy. "What will you do if you can't find a home?"

He shrugged his bare shoulders. "Let 'em go free."

"Allan," Billy pleaded.

"Let's think about it." He asked for the boy's number.

"No, just come by de fish market," the boy said. "Down by de pier." He sauntered away, the two puppies tucked into his shoulders, licking his brown skin.

"Allan," Billy said. "What will it take?"

He laughed. "I can't say, not here. But we don't need two dogs, do we?"

She jumped up and moved her halter-dressed body over to sit in his lap and whispered something in his ear. Fraser watched as the V slid sideways to let one breast come out for a quick visit. When he saw me watching him, he blushed and turned away.

"I said, I'll think about it." No more laughing. He pushed her off. She pouted and walked away from the table, toward the ladies' room.

"One more round?" Allan asked.

"No." I stood up and followed Billy. I heard Fraser trying to talk him out of it, too.

"You okay?" I asked Billy's feet in the stall beside mine.

"Yeah," she said. "Just a bit fragile when it comes to animals, I guess."

"Hard to turn down a puppy like that," I said. "Lots of paper-work. Shots. Responsibility."

People loved the formative stage. Puppies, babies, blossoms, cookie dough, new love. Was it biological? When you were looking at a young woman with her breasts popping out all over the place, how could you turn your gaze away and back to the person who loved you, who was married to you, who, in damp, muted Vancouver, made you happy?

After Billy and I left the bathroom, we plodded through the gravel back to the cottage to take turns showering, couple by couple. Fraser and I waited our turn on the porch, where he flaked out in the giant string hammock.

"You're right about thinking in the heat," he said. "I don't know how anything gets done."

"I guess you get used to it."

"Or else get up at four in the morning." He yawned, then belched.

"God, Fraser."

"Sorry."

"Can you believe the puppy scene back there?"

"I know. She's crazy about animals."

"She's crazy to be with that man."

"He's not so bad." Fraser's voice was quiet; he was almost asleep, just like that, rocking in the late afternoon breeze.

Allan *was* so bad. What was Billy doing with him? She gave off light like there was voltage from inside, like those plants that didn't need sun to grow. He was a dark and oppressive boot, squashing everything in his path.

"Okay, maties," Allan called before heading into their bedroom. "Your turn."

"Fraser," I said. "Let's go."

He didn't stir.

Then Billy came out, in only a towel, to tell us the bathroom was free.

"Oh, someone's sleepy!" she said. Of course, Fraser woke up when he heard her voice.

"Is it gelato time?"

"Not until you take a shower, stinky." Billy gave the hammock a little shove with her foot to get Fraser swinging.

"I'm going in," I said. "Stinky can come or not."

"Billy, get in here!" Allan bellowed from his bedroom.

"He wants you," I said. "Wink, wink."

She sighed. "He probably just can't find his shirt."

* * *

When we walked into the small gelato shop, I believed it could be the best in the world, mostly because of their glorious air-conditioning. I asked for a sample of a local red berry sorbet, which was tart and sweet and perfect paired with vanilla.

Allan asked for a sample of chocolate from the gelato maker, an

Italian who'd moved to the island ten years before, according to the guidebook.

"No samples," the man said.

"But how do I know what I want unless I try? *She* got a sample." Allan scowled at me.

"Everyone knows what chocolate tastes like. No one asks for a sample of chicken in a restaurant. You just order. No samples."

"I've eaten gelato all over the world, and nobody's refused me a sample."

"No samples." The man stood with his scoop ready.

Fraser stepped up to the dairy case. "I'll have vanilla."

Billy ordered what I had after she took a lick from my cone. Allan went out sulking. Then he sent Billy back in to buy him one. Chocolate.

Cones in hand, we strolled back to the cottage in the heavy night heat.

Fraser stopped to toss the last bit of his cone to a stray dog, and pulled me toward him for a kiss. "Having fun?"

"Good enough."

Hands on my hips, he pulled me into him so I could feel what kind of fun he wanted.

The bugs were starting to buzz. Billy and Allan were still heading toward the cottage, not touching. "What's on the agenda tonight?"

"This." Fraser pulled me tighter. "But Allan wants to go out for a drink or two first."

I groaned. "Really?" Any more time with that guy and I was going to implode. "I'm not up for it."

"I told him you wouldn't be. Neither is Billy. You two can hang, if that's okay? Get to know each other. I know she likes you, Sue. You can be like a mentor for her."

I felt my face burning a little at the hairline. "Mentor?"

"Nursey stuff. Woman stuff. Whatever."

"Fraser. We're on vacation." My heart was jumping. I kissed him lightly on the cheek. "That's fine. You two go and have your drinks. Billy and I will talk shop until the sun comes up."

* * *

As soon as the guys left us, Billy came out of her room in a tank top and short shorts.

"PJs at last," she said and sat at the kitchen table. "So good to have some girl time, isn't it?"

I agreed. I changed into a white cotton nightie, wishing I'd bought the baby dolls.

"You up for a game of Rummy?" Billy asked.

"I don't know how."

When she survived the shock, she brought a bottle of white rum to the table and told me she would show me how to play on one condition: that I get with it and try a rum and Coke. "Two firsts in one night for you," Billy said. "What a party!"

She dealt a hand and explained how it worked. I could smell her honeydew lipgloss.

"You think they're on the prowl?" she asked.

"What?"

"Fraser and Allan."

The thought hadn't crossed my mind. "Do you?"

She shrugged. "Wouldn't be the first time. For Allan, I mean."

"Really?"

"It's okay. I mean, I'm no angel." Suddenly, she was looking at me from behind her cards, just her snapping blue eyes showing.

I nodded, slowly, holding her gaze.

"What about you? And Fraser?"

"Oh, well." I looked at my cards, pretended to study them, arranged a few. "We're okay."

"What does that mean?"

"We're good."

Billy sniffed. "Good."

"Another beverage?" Was she trying to tell me that she knew something about Fraser that I didn't?

"You know, Allan has been an extra-big prick on this trip so far."

I sipped my drink, nodded slightly. White rum didn't taste all that bad.

"He gets so—so *parental* on me sometimes, that I just want to say, Fuck it. Never mind the attitude he's got about practically everything."

I nodded again. I was a nodding bird on the side of a drink. "How many years between you?"

It was the wrong thing to say. She looked at me, unsmiling. "It doesn't matter," she said. "He'd be like that with anyone."

"I don't know him," I said.

"Well, you've seen some classic Allan." She paused for another swig. "You guys seem so happy, in comparison."

I shook my head. "Believe me, Fraser's a little out of his element, too." I took another drink. "Maybe back in Calgary, everything will smooth itself out."

"I think this is the beginning of the end," she confided. "I want to see the world, you know, and Allan's already seen everything. When my friends come over, they don't even know what to say to him, he's so old, and settled. They feel like little kids around him."

"But what about school? Any decisions there?"

She shuffled the cards, then looked me straight in the eye. "Can you keep a secret?"

I nodded.

"I'm not actually in school right now. I've been saving up instead, for a trip to Spain."

"Without Allan knowing."

"Yep."

The little scoundrel. "And how will you tell him?"

"I won't. Just like Wendy in *Peter Pan*, I'll be gone in the night."

We'd abandoned the card game. She was holding the deck, looking dreamily into space.

"Want to sit out on the porch?" I asked. "It's cooler out there."

We took our tinkling drinks to the outside. Our towels and swimsuits were hanging over every surface except the hammock.

"Here," Billy said. "Let's sit sideways." She pulled open the hammock and sat her bum in first, legs over the edge.

"Think it'll hold?"

"Oh, sure," she said. "This is built for two."

I settled myself into the thousand strands of cotton that made up the loose weave.

"These can hold a Volkswagen," she told me. "I saw it on YouTube."

We started to swing, ever so slightly, outer arms behind our heads for pillows, our other hands holding our drinks. Slowly, with each rock of the hammock, our bodies began to slide into one another until there was no space between us. Our sides were in full contact, snug. I could feel a sort of vibration from her, as though her skin could barely contain her.

Or was that vibration from me?

We toasted again. "To rum!" Billy exclaimed, and giggled as the drink spilled on her chest.

"We need straws."

"No, I'll just finish this like a good girl," she said. "Bottoms up."

I drank mine down. My throat burned, as much from the Coke as the rum. I kept one ice cube into my mouth to chase the taste away.

Our glasses on the deck, we settled back into our nest.

"This is the best," Billy said. "Screw the guys."

A huge roll of thunder followed her words.

"Whoops! You made someone mad."

"Well, I mean it!" She shouted it to the sky. "To hell with them!"

The raindrops started like footsteps over us, on the tin roof above us, then quickly became a stampede.

"Wow. That came on fast."

"I love it." Billy laughed. "I love it!"

Our heads were touching, just behind the temples. We stared at the roof, at the sky, watched for lightning on the surface of the sea.

"Did you and Allan, you know, do it, on the balcony in Flores?"

Billy laughed quietly. "How'd you know?"

"Well," I said, "we were sitting outside, and . . ."

"Did you like what you heard?" she whispered into my ear.

"Uh-huh," I said. "I did."

We faced each other, and she pulled off her sticky tank top. Nothing on underneath but her coral choker. "Your turn," she said.

"I'm not the one who spilled her drink," I said. My nightie came off.

What was I doing? Next, we were nipple to nipple in a rainstorm, mouth to mouth, matching parts together. Electric. Honeydewed. Hot.

Allan was at the door, soaked to the skin. His round face glowed, red as a rubber ball. When he saw us, he grinned. We struggled to move apart in the cotton net.

"Interrupting something?"

"We're just getting comfortable," Billy said.

I grabbed my nightie and covered myself with it.

"Where's Fraser?"

"Dunno. Gotta piss. Don't go anywhere."

He stumbled into the bathroom, slamming the door behind him.

"Where were we?"

"Here," I said. I rubbed my palms across her nipples, and she moaned in my ear. But then I heard footsteps on the stairs.

Fraser, soaking wet, came in a moment later. I was out of the hammock; we both had managed to get our pyjamas on. I was breathless. "Did Allan come back here?"

Billy pointed at the bathroom door.

"Shit. He's going to be in deep shit, and us along with him."

"What for?"

"He—oh, my God." Fraser ran his hands through his drenched hair. "He broke a window in the gelato shop."

"Oh, no!" Billy hoisted herself out of the hammock and ran to the bathroom door. "Get out here, you idiot! You're in big trouble."

"Fuck off!"

"Were you with him?"

Fraser nodded. "But I couldn't catch him in time to stop him."

Billy came back to the porch. "Did anyone see?"

"I'm not sure. It was right when the storm started, so everyone was taking shelter. But who knows what people saw?"

"My God," I said. "This heat makes people do crazy things."

"We've got to get out of here, now. Find a taxi, a bus, whatever it takes, we just have to leave."

When Allan came out, Fraser told him his plan.

"No. Who the hell would take us at this time of night? Besides, we're here to see a croc, and tomorrow, we're going kayaking in the lagoon. And no one saw a thing. It's all okay."

He may have been talking about the rock he threw or the scene he walked in on. Kayaking? All I wanted was to lie around.

* * *

Spotting crocodiles is not a skill we need in the north; a log is a log in Canada, something to avoid when you're in a canoe, or compete on during logging sports. Early the next morning, we were in two plastic kayaks, doubles, seeking this live log out, to look at and photograph and brag about, because the men wanted survival tales. Something more exciting than starfish and nurse sharks and gelato.

The crime of the night before wasn't mentioned, but I sensed a tension between the guys.

Billy and I were united: we didn't want to see a crocodile. But it was a holiday, we'd be on the ocean, it was our last hurrah, the thing to do. If we didn't go, we might've been together for the whole morning. My marriage needed the buffer zone of the men. My body ached with what remained unfinished.

I saw the crocodile first, motionless, sunning itself on the muddy bank. I didn't say anything, just watched it to see if it was sleeping. When we eased closer, I nudged Fraser with my paddle; he looked at me, and I pointed out the monster.

He was just about to whisper to Allan when Billy saw it, too, and started screaming. Of course the croc started moving and quickly slid into the water and disappeared; at the same time, our two kayaks collided. Then Billy, screaming even more, fell into the lagoon.

What happened next was film-worthy. We shouted at her to grab on to the boat, but she was panicking, splashing around as if the croc already had her by the foot.

Allan yelled, "For God's sake, get out of there!"

Our kayak was closer to her, and before I could think properly about the possibility of being pulled in by her—never reach for a drowning person—I turned around in my seat, grasped Billy's arms, and pulled her onto the centre of our boat. She was between Fraser and me, on her belly and hysterical, lifting her legs out of the water.

"It's coming, I almost have my period and I know it can smell me! I saw a show on TV! Oh, my God, I hate this. I hate this!" The kayak rocked with her sobs.

"Billy," I said. "Calm down, now. You have to turn around and sit up." I offered her my hand.

Fraser scanned the surface for the crocodile. "It's long gone. Billy, it's okay."

"Billy!" Allan was shouting again. "Get it together and turn around. I'm coming up beside you. You have to move into my boat."

"I can't! Allan, I can't! I'll fall in again, and I'll die!"

"Billy! Stop your blubbering and turn around, or I swear, I will just fucking flip!"

At his bark, she took my hand and pulled herself up on all fours. Although she was still crying, she managed to stay focused enough so that when we were next to Allan's kayak, she was able to step into the front seat.

"Holy shit," Fraser said, after Billy's stifled sobs subsided. "That was insane."

"What the hell happened? How did you end up in the fucking water?"

"Allan. She slipped." Fraser shrugged.

Allan muttered something.

Fraser leaned forward. "What are you saying?"

"Just that she does this kind of shit all the time. I'm sick of it."

Billy was curled, chest to knees, her body protecting her heart.

"Enough, Allan." Fraser's voice cracked. "She's totally upset right now, can't you see that?"

"Let's go." Allan started paddling furiously and the kayak jerked toward the mouth of the lagoon. Billy, up front, was in no shape to paddle.

We followed him silently and made our way back toward the pier. When we could see the dock, Fraser touched my arm with his paddle, then pointed at the dock.

People were waiting: the man in a white T-shirt and neon green shorts who'd rented us our kayaks, and three men dressed in sand-coloured pants and shirts. Police.

Allan looked back at Fraser. We stopped paddling. Our two kayaks slowed. Choppy waves jostled us. My stomach rolled.

"Oh, shit," Fraser said.

Allan looked first at Fraser and then at me. "Guess we've got to face our demons."

"What do we do?" Fraser asked.

"Confess," Billy said in a congested voice. "Get your story straight and get it over with."

"Yeah," Allan said. "Come to think of it, the little girl's bang on. Better to just lay it all out."

He smirked at me. My heart stopped.

"Sue," he said. "Why don't you go first?"

The King Is Dead

There was little chance we'd see any loon chicks that morning on the lake. It was the middle of summer, and I knew the babies had been growing for months already. But my nephew, Sammy, age five and three-quarters, wanted to look all the same—at the end of our family's beach, he'd found a few dark feathers with white spots. I didn't have the heart to tell him they were most likely from a long-dead chick.

Sammy and I set out for a trip in the old green canoe, after he'd pleaded with his mother, my sister Donna, to let him go. She relented only after I promised to make him wear his sun hat and lay down my life for him if we tipped—I practically had to demonstrate my CPR skills.

He turned his blond, curly-haired head around to face me as I pushed us away from the dock. "Auntie Trish, what did you call the canoe when you were a little kid?"

"The pea-green pod."

Sammy laughed as if he hadn't heard me say it just ten minutes earlier. "And we're the peas, right?"

Donna made him sit in the bottom of the canoe because he was less likely to fall overboard from there. We'd had to do the same thing when our father—a man I termed "The Emp"—took Donna and me out to hunt for bullfrogs when we were kids. On one of those frog hunts, Donna and I decided to trail our fingers in the water on the same side of the canoe at the same time, and we ended up in the lake just a few feet from the dock. It shouldn't have been a big deal; Donna and I thought it was hilarious, and we'd bobbed around in our keyhole life jackets, kicking and splashing. But Dad started yelling at us to keep our heads up, as if we could do anything else, our heads framed in padded canvas, and next thing I knew, he was screaming for our mother. "Dee! Help! Help!" She came rushing right into the water, arms flailing, to save us. We didn't need saving, but she'd acted as though the lake held electric eels or a crazy undertow. She didn't catch her breath until we were safely on the dock. Then she helped Dad turn the canoe over and pull it back to shore. He repeated over and over, "I'm sorry, Dee, I'm sorry. It's all my fault." Our bossy, headstrong father was sobbing.

"Your father needs a rest," our mother had said and helped him up the stairs to the cottage as though he were wounded.

Sammy and I were out a hundred feet from shore. From that distance I could barely see a cottage at all; the cedars in front of it had grown into one another to form a dull green cloud. My mother was away at a local day spa with some friends from Ottawa, a celebration for a woman whose cancer had gone into remission, but The Emp was behind that cloud, holding down a Muskoka chair, a highball in his hand.

I paddled as little as possible, just one J-stroke every few minutes, while Sammy looked for loons, and then I let my paddle rest across the gunwales and watched the water drip back, dimpling the flat surface. I'd always loved this lake best in the morning, before anyone else could ruin the day with their rules about water safety or their hangover gloom. I used to wake up early and swim, unencumbered, before my parents were up; just in case my mother asked if I'd worn my life jacket, I always left it soaking in the water, ready to show her.

Sammy was squirming around like someone needing to pee, although he'd gone before we set off. I asked him why he was so wiggly.

"Because we're on an adventure!" He opened his small blue backpack and pulled out four plastic people. "Look who I brought!" He held up one of the figures. "You gave me these, back when I was little-little."

The pirates. Wow. I'd bought him the pirates the last time I'd seen him—two Decembers ago, when Donna had brought him to Toronto to see *The Nutcracker*. We'd met in the Eaton Centre, in front of a toy store, and Sammy was crying because he wanted the hundred-dollar Playmobil pirate ship, and he wanted it right then and there. The crowd curdled around us; I could barely breathe in my puffy coat. My hair was full of typical winter mall static, my fingers were cracked from the cold, and my lips were shredded.

"Looking good," Donna said. Donna's curls lay flat due to the toque she'd stuffed in her coat pocket. On her thigh was a smear of snot at Sammy's nose level.

"You, too." At one point our words would have carried irony, but we pretended we meant it. "Should we grab a bite to eat now?" The only thing I knew about kids: keep them fed and things go better.

Sammy then spent the whole half-hour in the food court driving French fries through ketchup drifts, making vroom-vroom noises while Donna and I caught up.

The food court was crammed with dozens of little kids all jumping out of their skin, so hyped up for the big day. I remembered that can't-wait feeling so well, and I missed it. On impulse, I hopped to my feet and told Donna and Sammy to keep themselves parked, and ran down to the toy store to buy him that pirate ship.

The look on Sammy's face when I handed it to him was worth the frown on Donna's.

"What do you say?" she prompted.

"It's awesome!" Sammy had cried.

What was truly awesome was that this little boy remembered that the pirates were a gift from me. He lined them up on the canoe seat in front of him, faces staring into the clear blue sky because they wouldn't stay standing; my solo paddling skills weren't what they used to be. I hadn't been in a canoe for three years, the length of time I'd been away from the cottage.

Sammy, the pirates, and I scoured the lake's edge, trying to avoid the big rocks marked by floating bleach bottles. He was so happy, he was singing made-up songs, every now and then adding a *matey* and an *Arrr,* as if he never came out on the water.

Sammy, Donna, and her husband, Mitch, live half a mile up the road, inland. Spending so much time by the water when we were kids made my sister want to move to the area; Mitch commutes to the outskirts of Ottawa for some kind of boring telecom work while she stays in the country with Sammy, who's just finished kindergarten. When The Emp inherited the cottage, we spent our summers at the lake.

"Do you come out on the lake very often?"

"No, Mommy's afraid I'll drown," Sammy said matter-of-factly. "She knows a lot of stories about kids who died in water."

The same old paranoia, coming down the line. "And you're not scared?"

"Oh, no," he said. "I've got this life jacket. Plus, you're here."

His trust and obedience were kind of sweet. He was a kid who didn't even try to go hatless or upset his mother.

What did he know about me? I'd been a scrawny, jumpy, sugar-loving kid, then a sullen teen with a hate-on for pretty much anything except for my own take on style—wearing lingerie as clothing, lacy underwear over street clothes, an upside-down crucifix—and I'd turned into a scrawny, jumpy, sugar-loving tattooed adult with my own company, designing websites for people who want an edge to their image—*Artful Darkness*. Nice of Donna, in a way, to have kept the stories of Auntie Trish to herself.

✳ ✳ ✳

Sammy and I returned to the dock, empty-handed and hungry. Donna greeted us by throwing her arms around Sammy as if she'd been away from him for weeks. "You need more sunscreen," she told him. "Come on, let's go up."

We climbed the stairs and discovered that The Emp had a visitor. "You remember George, Trish?" The Emp asked.

I nodded. I guessed the family was still buying corn on the cob and tomatoes from his farm. He was sitting in the other Muskoka chair on the deck. Donna disappeared into the cottage.

"Gidday, kiddo," George said. "How's the fishing?"

Sammy cocked his head and put his hands on his hips. "We weren't fishing, we were searching for loons."

George laughed and looked at me. "Looks like you found one."

"Sammy, come here and give your old grandpa a hug." Sammy ran over to The Emp and nearly sent his highball flying. "Careful, now, my boy. Careful."

"Long time no see," I said to George. "How's it going?"

"Can't complain." He lifted his beer. "And what do we have here?"

Donna brought out a bowl of nuts, some crackers and cheese, and a jelly sandwich for Sammy, who snatched it and headed back down to the beach, announcing his intention to make a sandcastle. Donna looked at the spray in her hand. "Wait! I forgot your sunscreen!"

While my sister did her mother-thing, I settled in for a chat on the deck and George told us why he could afford to visit, evidently a rare event. At the beginning of the summer, his wife and kids had gone to the East Coast, to visit her family until Labour Day. "It's a good thing," he said. "Time on my hands for once." I didn't believe him. His shoulders were sad—even with all that meat on his bones, his shoulders looked thin and empty.

"Hey, those things hurt?" George was pointing at my tattooed shoulder, the morning glory vines wrapping around from my pecs to the bottom of my shoulder blade.

"Not much."

The Emp said, "Bring the good man another beverage, Patricia."

I took a deep breath: nothing had changed. My father hadn't asked a single question about my life since my arrival, and while my mother had been chatty, Donna ignored me and went about doing Sammy stuff. I'd always been the outsider, estranged from them, not part of their secret family club. We were right back to the usual patterns. Sure, I'd go get George another beer.

Donna came back and we sat and shot the breeze for a few more minutes, marvelling at the run of decent weather, the low number of mosquitoes.

After he finished his beer, George needed to use the bathroom. He started to rise from his chair, but it wouldn't let him go. He tried again, grunting and laughing, with no luck. George had really wedged himself into that Muskoka chair. He was completely jammed in. "You attached to this here chair, Bob?" he asked my father. "Might have to bust me out of her."

"Oh, don't worry, we'll get you out." The Emp directed Donna and me in his teacherly voice that was beginning to slur a little. "Each of you hold down an arm now, while George stands up. These chairs are awful. Damned nuisances."

It worked. Freed from the chair, George shook himself off like he'd won a fight, then limped to the bathroom.

"Thank God we're outside," I whispered. George gave off a blend of cow shit, diesel fumes, and farts. "Pee-ew."

"Hush, now," The Emp said. "He works hard." He put on his

glasses and picked up the *Globe and Mail*'s Review section. Soon he was making a sound I recognized: a half-whistle, half-hum that meant he was feeling no pain.

I remembered Bob Hudson, a.k.a. The Emp, as a successful man in every way, including his success, if you'd call it that, at getting completely sloshed on a daily basis. It seemed he was still good at it. I came up with "The Emp," my name for him, as a teenager, and I'd referred to him as The Emp ever since. When I mentioned it to Donna, I said the name referred to his proclamations, his putting on airs and accents, like an aristocrat—short for The Emperor. The one who wears no clothes? she'd asked. Sure, I'd said. If the shoe fits. It could also be short for Empties. Donna stuck with "Dad." The good daughter who'd stuck.

I was just coming out of a pretty bleak period—a dark and rainy spring, a bad breakup, my friends dating decent people and plotting their futures. The guy who'd dumped me, like most of the guys I'd attracted, had taken my darker look to mean hard "partier." Yet I'd always been too afraid; I worried that it would be like enticing tapeworms to come out through my mouth with a saucer of milk at my lips—the addict rising from deep inside, wanting to be fed. The last guy quipped, "I didn't know I was signing up for a church lady. You have twelve tattoos. You like Rage Against the Machine, for fuck sakes!" He called my look "false advertising." Needless to say, I hadn't found a decent match.

With George rescued, Donna left the deck and descended the dozen steps to the beach to skip stones with Sammy. It was like being on holiday for her. Whenever our parents were at the cottage, Donna came over every day.

"Want some cheddar?" I asked The Emp. "Or did you already have lunch?"

"I'm fine," he said. "Sister took care of me."

I took up the steel wool and continued scrubbing down the

barbecue. We'd cooked up some tandoori chicken breasts I brought from the city only on Mom's condition that the grill would be pristine again the next day.

"Just turn her up to five hundred and walk away," George said, returning from the loo. "Best clean you'll ever get."

"Is that so?" I kept at it. George sat himself down on another, easier-to-exit chair. The Emp had gone quiet, his pink face contemplative under his bushy white head of hair—good hair even at seventy years old, no messy-look hair product required. He looked smaller than he had on my last visit to Ottawa, but I put it down to the oversized chair he was in.

"What's the big thing at the farm these days?" I asked George, as if a century-old farm made quick decisions on crops and livestock. I wondered if organic had hit that part of the country yet. I handed him another Molson's.

"Oh, same old corn and beef. After sixty years of farming, Dad won't stray from those. But there's a couple fields in the back corner where I'm growing buckwheat, kind of an experiment. A cereal company pays decent money for the stuff. Purely a cash crop, I guess."

"I used to sell buckwheat. Raw and toasted. When I worked at the health food store."

"Yeah, it's a hippie thing." George squinted at my nose. "See you took your bull ring out."

I ignored this brilliant observation. "It's high in protein, compared with other grains."

"You ever eat it?"

"Sure." I'd only ever eaten it once, at a friend's geodesic dome. They served it like porridge with soya butter and soya sauce, and I couldn't get the burnt, bitter taste off my tongue for two days.

"I'll stick to other protein, thanks," George said and dug through the bowl of mixed nuts with his dirty hands, rooting out the cashews. "You want some, Bob?" But The Emp couldn't answer; he'd passed out.

Just as we noticed his condition, we heard excitement from the lake.

"Grandpa! Grandpa!" It was Sammy, yelling from the dock. "We caught a bullfrog!"

The Emp's head was bent toward his chest.

"Good job," George yelled back. "Hold on tight!"

My father didn't stir.

"Napping, Bob?" George nudged The Emp's foot with his own. "He okay? Heart okay?"

"Oh, I think so," I said. "He's been drinking his medicine all day."

"Ah, shit." George chuckled. "I shoulda known that. I thought it was water at first, all fancy-like with the lemon. The way he was guzzling."

"The only water he gets is in the ice."

The Emp was slowly slumping over; his top half was about to fall sideways out of the chair. George jumped up to catch him.

"You want me to put him to bed?"

"I guess we'd better."

Donna had come up to check on things. George picked up my father like he was a sack of potatoes, hefted him into the cottage, and laid him down, tenderly, on the old feather mattress in the bedroom closest to the front door. As I shifted him away from the edge of the bed, I was surprised to feel how bony The Emp's limbs were, how insubstantial they felt under his grey cotton slacks.

At that moment Sammy yelled from the dock again. "Mommy! Come help me! The pool noodles are floating away!"

"Oh, bloody hell," Donna muttered.

A fake inner Brit surfaced when she panicked, something else she inherited from The Emp. He always liked to act British, used to go days with an affected accent, a slight tea-time tightness to his voice. Maybe a by-product of the gin, a distillation of Her Majesty's royal juniper berries, but more likely it was a way for him to feel distinguished among the neighbours in Ottawa, who were senior civil servants or professors. A high school history teacher was not a prof. At one point, apparently, he could have taken things further and done his PhD, but then Donna came along, and then me, and after all (although this is not a part of the official story), in my opinion, he was busy dedicating his free time to the bottle.

I could feel the day settling into my shoulder muscles, knotting them up. "Thanks for stopping by," I said to George, who stood on the deck, finishing his beer. A light wind had begun to blow, and on it, the scent of the wild roses growing along the dirt lane. I decided to walk with him out to the main road. We kept a leisurely, work-boot pace.

"You don't miss it around here? Big city's not too much for you?"

"No, it isn't," I said. It wasn't true. I missed the lake so much. The city offered me chances, diversity, stimulation, but the lake was *my* medicine; it settled me down.

"Donna's pretty happy living here, seems like," George said. "Nice little family. Good mother."

"Yeah. Maybe a little over the top with the safety drills."

George slowed down and lowered his voice. "Well, now, you can never be too careful. After Patrick and all."

Who was Patrick? "What do you mean?"

He jerked his head to the side and looked at me hard. "Oh. Well, then. I better be off." He looked embarrassed. He hoisted up his jeans and turned toward his farm. "Give my best to your mother."

Probably a little dotty, mixing up stories. Or maybe it was the beer at work, making him forget that I hadn't been around in years and no longer knew the local stories.

"Will do," I called. "Good luck with the buckwheat."

✳ ✳ ✳

Back at the cottage, I went to check if The Emp was still alive. Not choking on his own spew, able to breathe. Good enough. I lay down on the couch to try to fight off a headache that was beginning to build.

Alcohol was an addiction, and addicts needed empathy. And I felt it—for people I didn't know, at least. I knew that people were hurting everywhere, and needed to soothe their brokenness with whatever they could get. The thing was, my father was not suffering. He had a wife who dedicated *her* life to creating a magazine-worthy home—albeit, for me, a claustrophobic one—two kids who hadn't fucked up in any substantial way, a job with enough money to let him keep the cottage, and seemingly rock-solid health despite his dirty habit. He had a good life. It should have added up to something better than his regular obliteration.

Donna had turned into Mom, pretending the man didn't have a problem, and I didn't blame her: she was a lot closer to our parents, and now with a boy who needed grandparents, I could see why she'd rather live as if things were rosy. Sammy and my father loved each other. Yesterday The Emp must've played ten rounds of Go Fish! and even read Sammy a story. Despite deliberately leaving all this behind, I envied Donna her full life.

As for me, when I wasn't working, or had no new boyfriend in the bed, my days were empty vessels; I'd begun to think that getting tattoos was intimate—the buzz, the pain, the blood, the scarring— and at least I was left with something I wanted to see again. I was only twenty-seven, but I was lonely. I was starting to think I would become one of those women on the streetcar who tell strangers about their breakfast, just to talk.

I didn't think of Sammy often before the day in the mall. But when he was with me in the canoe, I felt something completely new: he was mine. Not that I owned him. I guess you could call it kinship. He was my nephew; I was his auntie. Maybe that relationship could mean more than just buying him presents.

* * *

After a few minutes, Sammy came into the cottage and stood on the mat, soaking wet and shivering, still in his life jacket.

"What's up, matey?"

"The frog swam away, and we lost the blue noodle." He began to whimper.

I got up to help. "You don't want to take that thing off?" He stepped into the antique Care Bears towel I was holding open. He smelled like coconut SPF 100 and fish skin.

"I'm going back down," he said.

I rubbed his little arms to warm him up.

"That was my favourite noodle!" He grumbled some more.

"Oh, well, it's just gone down the lake a bit. We'll get it later. You and me in the pea-green pod, okay?" It sounded more like naptime than canoe time. Did kids still nap?

"Mommy's doing that already."

I looked out the window over the sink to the lake below. Donna had managed to get the canoe into the water and up alongside the dock. I lifted Sammy up onto the counter. "Let's watch her!"

He was still shaking, his taut muscles vibrating against my shoulder like a washing machine.

"She wouldn't let me go," he whined. "I wanted to go along!"

"She'll be right back," I told him. How could I teach him to take that whine out of his voice?

Sammy sat on the counter, his feet in the kitchen sink, and we both observed Donna from above. We were watching closely when she stepped into the wrong side of the boat and fell into the lake.

* * *

Donna has cerebral palsy, just a mild case that affects one side of her body. The cord was wrapped around her neck at birth and deprived her brain of oxygen for minutes. After multiple surgeries on her left arm and leg, she's been left with one smaller hand and one smaller foot—lucky, in comparison to most others with CP. She holds her arm like it's a wounded paw and takes shorter steps so the foot doesn't drag her down, but otherwise, she's totally okay.

Naturally, she's had to make concessions, and so has her family. There were times during our childhood when I felt like one of those rats that turned to horses in Cinderella, pulling her royal carriage—the little red wagon did get up to a decent speed with a dose of younger-sibling anger as fuel.

"Trish! Trish!" Donna started calling to us before she could see we were on the way down to help her. "Throw me a bloody life preserver!" More with the panic, British-style.

She was flapping around, perfectly fine, but stressing herself out working to get the canoe turned upright. A boa of weeds ringed her neck. I threw her the life jacket to complete the ensemble.

"The blasted paddles!" Donna yelled. "They're floating away!" She held on to the life jacket and started kicking her way toward them.

At this point, our mother arrived home. I caught a glimpse of a pearly silver car pulling out of the driveway as she floated down the steps in her post-spa bliss, wearing a shapeless sage green tunic.

"Donna's swimming, is she?" Mom asked in a smiley voice. "Hello, dear Sammy. Hello, Patricia."

"Not swimming, Grandma," Sammy said. "She was chasing the noodles and then she tipped out of the canoe and now the paddles are gone, too."

Mom looked at me for confirmation, the worry back on her face. I nodded. "Business as usual."

"Where's your father?"

"Napping."

She sighed. Spa time was over. "Sammy, will you come with me in the pedal boat, once you find your sun hat? We are going on a rescue mission."

Sammy cheered. "Another adventure!"

Donna had given up and was climbing the ladder at the end of the dock, red-faced and panting, picking weeds out of her bathing suit. The green canoe was face down in the lake.

"Hello, dear," Mom said. "Are you all right?"

And although my sister was clearly not all right, judging by her rate of breathing and the pissy expression she wore, she followed our code of conduct: never alarm our mother, never make sudden gestures, or talk about adventures we've had, never admit to bodily harm. Donna simply nodded.

* * *

The Emp wasn't a bad guy. He didn't hit us, didn't wake us up in the middle of the night to beat us, like my friend's mother had, calling them little shits and worse, as if they were being bad while they slept. He never touched me *down there*, never mortally wounded anyone. But still, it was hard for me. I had to learn to lie, for him and for me. I never took rides with him after 3:00 PM, never volunteered my daddy for pickup after dances or shows. I took to pouring out his bottles, filling them with coloured water, throwing tantrums about it, leaving Alcoholics Anonymous pamphlets out for him to stumble over, the whole nine yards. I pleaded with my mother to help, but she wouldn't entertain the idea that anything was dire enough to seek help. Wouldn't want word getting out, now, would we?

* * *

After Sammy and my mother were tucked into the pedal boat and pushing toward the runaway paddles and noodles, Donna and I waded into the lake and worked together to get the canoe turned over, then into shore.

"Doesn't this remind you of that day we tipped with The Emp?" I asked her when we were resting on plastic chairs on the beach beside Sammy's sandcastle.

She shook her head. "I don't really remember it."

"Really? The day he cried?"

Donna avoided my gaze and started rattling on about the high water level and the petition going around about banning gas motors on the lake.

I pressed on. "You really don't remember?"

She stood up. "No, I don't. Now will you please help me take these chairs away from the edge of the lake in case those clouds mean business?"

Bulbous clouds were gathering at the far end of the lake, but it was still sunny and clear at our place. I dropped the memory talk and helped her, and then said I was going back up to check on The Emp. I really just wanted to take a Tylenol and lie down again for a few minutes.

"I'll come, too," she said. "Should we try to get him up? Wash his face, change his shirt, you know, while Mom is out?"

"Not a chance," I said. We climbed the stairs, me letting her go first, as always. "He's a big boy, Donna. It's not up to us any more."

I tried to imagine the future. Who would take care of him if Mom were to go before he did? Not me. I could not see myself swabbing his bony, pseudo-aristocratic ass with a Wet One. No. Not my department.

He was lying on his back like a coffined body, hands on his belly, cheeks flushed, that familiar, sweetly-acrid scent escaping his pores.

"At least we should open the window," Donna said. "It smells in here."

She crawled onto the bed and reached over The Emp to the window: the cottage was built when people were shrunken versions of what they are now, when a vacation house's bedroom was a cubbyhole and people built according to how much cold, hard cash they had in hand. All the windows were old storm windows from an even older house, hinged on their top edge and held open by hooks suspended from the rafters of the unfinished ceiling.

When there was air flow, we closed his door and began cleaning up the kitchen.

"Oh, hey, maybe you know," I said as I swept the floor. "George mentioned something that happened to a boy named Patrick?"

Donna stopped wiping the table for a second.

"Did you know him?"

She turned to the stove and attacked its surface. "You'll have to ask Mom."

I heard Mom and Sammy stomping up the stairs. Donna dropped her rag and raced out to meet them. I kept sweeping. There was enough sand on that floor to build a castle.

My mother came into the kitchen, her sage green tunic soaked up to her hips. "Well," she said. "We found everything down by the Murphy place." She was speaking slowly, melodically, the way she used to talk when she wanted to distract us from something. Like steering us away from an accident on the road, saying, "Let's all go over here for ice cream, shall we?"

"Nearly time for dinner! I brought some lovely tomatoes and basil home from the market near the spa, and I thought we could start with a bruschetta. Or, Patricia, would you rather make one of your famous Greek salads?"

Wow, she was really going back in time; I hadn't made a Greek salad in years. "Mom," I said. "Who's Patrick?"

"Who? Oh." She cleared her throat. She pulled out a kitchen chair and sat down. "Well."

She sat staring out at the lake. I could hear Donna and Sammy on the deck, discussing the reasons why he couldn't stuff three cookies into his mouth at the same time.

"Are you okay, Mom?"

"Yes, Trish. I'm okay." Her voice was barely audible. "But I think—yes, you'd better come out on the deck, before your father wakes up."

I stuck the broom back in the closet and found Mom and Donna outside on the deck, having a mumbled conversation that stopped when I arrived. They were sitting at the oval plastic table with their hands folded in front of them. They looked as if they'd seen a ghost; their faces were pale and they wouldn't look at me directly.

"Sit down," they said in unison. A team approach. I sat down in the same chair The Emp had passed out in.

"Where's Sammy?" I suddenly wanted him with me; I needed a comrade.

"Castle town," Donna pointed toward the beach.

He was struggling to manoeuvre his sand pails, wearing that stupid life jacket. She probably made him wear it on rainy days.

"So," Mom said. "George was here." She was smiling, but it was more of her fake niceness.

"So who's Patrick?"

My mother looked at her lap.

"Donna, will you please tell me who Patrick is?"

There was a long pause. "Well," Donna said. "He was . . ." She looked at Mom.

"He was a darling boy," Mom finished quietly. "You would have loved him."

I was confused. "Yeah, but who was he?"

She wouldn't look at me. "He was my little boy."

"Wait a second." Something about the way she and Donna kept darting looks at each other was making me sweat. "Are you saying that he—that you have another child?" I looked to Donna for help. "We have a brother?"

She nodded. "Neither of us knew him."

My right eyelid began to twitch. A brother? I had a brother? The questions tumbled out. "What do you mean, *knew* him? Where is he? What happened?"

"He was playing in the water," Mom said. "I was in the hospital, with a newborn Donna, and your father was at home with him."

Donna leaned over and down to get a better view of Sammy, even though we could hear him singing.

"What, you mean he's—he's dead?"

"He died that day," Donna said. "Five years old. Sammy's age."

"Oh, my God." I'd had a brother, and lost him. "Why didn't you tell me?" Then I got it: The Emp. It felt as though chainmail had dropped over my shoulders. "He was drunk, wasn't he?"

"No," Mom said. "No, he wasn't." She spoke too loudly. "It was an accident."

"As if," I said.

My mother was adamant. "Your father didn't drink back then. I mean, he had a beer or two in the afternoons, but he wasn't—he didn't drink, like now." She closed her eyes for a moment, as if to summon her stronger self. "We didn't want either of you to carry this around. A dead brother can haunt you forever. God knows I know that, with my brother taken by that car crash. And I didn't want you to be afraid of water. So, we just pretended there had been ... no Patrick. We focused on raising you two instead, in the best way we could."

"Incredible." To think I'd had a brother.

"Bob loved him so much," Mom went on. She rose slowly and walked over to where she'd left her purse on the railing, pulled out her wallet, and took a photo from within its folds. "Look, this is the two of them, together, just a few months before—before he was taken from us."

I looked closely at the photo. A young Emp was holding a small blond kid on his knee like he was playing Santa. A boy with the same eye shape as him. Patrick. They were smiling, as if someone were making a puppet dance behind the camera. Happy. Living a good life. Alive, a hundred percent.

Patrick looked a bit like Donna had when she was young, but even more like Sammy, singing Sammy, down at the edge of the lake.

"I can't believe this," I said. "Why would you keep this from me?"

"Trish, they did the best they could." Donna had her arms folded, her small hand tucked behind the good one.

My sister had known. Everyone had known. "When did you find out?"

Donna looked away. "Just after I had Sammy, Dad kind of—well, he had a sort of a breakdown. Mom had to tell me why."

"I see. And you just wanted to keep me completely in the dark." Now I was pacing the deck. "What, like forever?"

"Can you imagine how hard it must have been? Coming home with a newborn, and losing a son? Give Mom a break, will you?"

"I'm sorry, Mom. It must be a horrible thing to lose a child."

She sat back in her chair and looked at me, surprised, I think, by my generosity.

"But it's just too unfuckingbelievable that you told Donna and not me."

"Trish!" Donna said. "Keep your voice down." She leaned to see Sammy again.

"Did the police come? Was there an investigation?"

Mom shook her head. "There was nothing to investigate. A little boy drowned in a lake, Trish. A tragedy. No one to blame."

"Except Beefeater. Or was it Jack Daniels? What was it then, Mom?"

My mother just stared at the photo.

I stared into the white cedars all around us, keeping us hidden from the world. They were full of cedar seeds, tight lime-green buds that The Emp used to pelt us with when he'd had a few, stinging our bare arms and legs despite our pleas for him to stop. He'd laughed; he'd wanted to make us hurt.

Sammy was belting out "Frère Jacques" below, really letting the lake have it. Donna wouldn't look at me. But she couldn't, really, could she? She was always head-cranked toward the beach, making sure the orange of Sammy's life jacket was still in view.

My mother's lips were trembling. "Trish. Your father was not a drinker back then. He wasn't. He was a sweet man who wanted a simple, sweet life, and then his only son died."

"His only son," I repeated. "It ruined him, is what you're saying."

She nodded, teary-eyed. "I thought having other children would help him."

"Yeah, well, that turned out nicely, didn't it? The love's just poured out of him ever since."

"See, I knew we shouldn't have told her," Donna said to Mom. "She's too damned selfish to even get it!" Then she turned to me. "Do you know that they were worried every second we were here at the lake, but they didn't want us to miss out on all this?"

Mom put up her hand to stop Donna. "It's okay. Trish has a right to be angry. She's always felt like she's had the short end of the stick, no matter how hard I tried." Her voice broke. "I tried to make your life the best it could be, but I failed. You've just abandoned us, living your perfect life in Toronto, and I don't know where I went wrong."

"Really, you don't know? You lied to me my whole life. How's that for starters?"

"You're such a little bitch!" Donna yelled. "You don't deserve any of what she's done for you. Always the baby, always special little Trish, the weird but talented one doing her own thing in the big city, too busy to care about her family. Why should she have told you about Patrick? Would it have made any difference to you and your holier-than-everyone attitude? No. It would just make you hate Dad even more."

Mom put her hands over her ears and began to rock a little, eyes shut tight. Donna wasn't finished.

"In fact, why are you even here now? We're all beneath you, isn't that what you've always thought? That we aren't good enough to be your family?"

Sammy kept on singing, "Ding dang dong" over and over again, under what had become a cloudy sky.

Donna's words stung, even if she was onto something: I did have to get away from there. But as much as I wanted to peel out and head back to Toronto right that minute, I couldn't leave. I had to face my father. I wanted to hear what The Emp had to say.

I went to sit in my car. The sky had started to spit. I began to move one hand over the other, stroking my skin, a strategy called "Pet the Bunny," a calm-down technique I hadn't needed since I left therapy.

* * *

There was no bruschetta for dinner, no famous Greek salad. While I was still in the car, all windows and doors closed, Donna called Sammy up from the beach. I stared at him and imagined it was Patrick I was seeing, imagined him into the part of my life I'd already lived through. Big brother at my birthday parties. Big brother teasing me about boyfriends. Big brother driving me places.

Eventually I left the car and went inside. Somebody had made a stack of grilled cheese sandwiches and left them on a plate in the middle of the table. I wasn't hungry, but Sammy had grabbed three triangles and was zooming them through a dune of ketchup, just like he'd done in the mall. Donna had the Uno cards out. She said Mom had gone to lie down.

I went to my room. Our heads—Mom and mine—would be nearly touching, separated by only a few inches of plywood and panelling. I heard Donna and Sammy playing Uno at the coffee table in the living room just outside my door, and above that peaceful sound, The Emp, snoring in the far bedroom.

I walked past the game, pulled a chair in from the kitchen table, and carefully closed the door. I sat beside the bed. "Dad," I said. "Get up."

When he didn't respond I took water from the glass on the bedside table and flicked it at him. "Get up, will you?"

His cheeks twitched with each spray, until he turned over and moaned. I moved on to clapping in his ear and finally he thrashed himself awake.

"Dad," I said quietly. "I know."

The Emp sat up and rubbed his ruddy face.

"What?" He tried to focus on me. "What are you talking about?"

"Patrick," I said. "I know about Patrick."

He opened his red-rimmed eyes and looked right at me before sinking onto his back again. "Donna tell you? Or your mother?"

"George told me first, they told me the rest."

His voice was raspy and dry. "My little son. Patrick."

Then it dawned on me: Patrick; Patricia. I was named after this dead boy. Their way of keeping a little bit of him alive.

"You were trying for another boy," I said. "And got me instead."

After a moment, he said, "Yes."

The Emp said yes.

Twenty-seven years of being an outsider, in that one word. *Yes.* I'd been a replacement for Patrick. But not a good one. Not good enough.

"And you were drunk, right?" I whispered. "The day Patrick died."

He struggled onto his elbows and sat up again. For what was the first time in years, The Emp was really looking at me. He nodded. "I'm sorry," he whispered.

I could hear Sammy exclaiming about the sunset from the living room. My mother's bed creaked and I could make out the shuffle of her flip-flops. The show must go on.

I couldn't wait to tell them the truth; it would feel so good. My brother was dead because of this man. A lie lay buried in the foundation of this family because of this man.

I had to tell them the truth, didn't I?

Didn't I? Yet.

Yet, if I did, the most likely scenario would be destruction.

Donna would flip out, maybe pull Sammy away from his grandpa.

Mom would be hurt, never forgive me.

The family would distance themselves from me even further.

I wouldn't get to see Sammy.

I leaned in close to The Emp's face again. "Who else knows?"

His nose was running. "No one," he whispered. "Other than God."

* * *

I left my father lying in his own mess and went to find Sammy. The weather had turned fair again, but the lake was still mottled with choppy waves. Donna and Mom were sitting on the deck, teary faces staring at a decent sunset, cups of tea on the table. Sammy was back on the beach, padded in his foam and nylon shield.

I ran down the steps to him. Sammy, my little not-brother stand-in.

At the shoreline stood his creation: a whole fortified city, complete with walls and moat and little pirates peeking from around the corners.

"Look at my castle town!"

"Amazing." He'd made a very cool town. I knelt down to get closer.

"This is where the king lives," Sammy told me, pointing at the biggest castle, nearest the lake. "It's strongest."

The castle was already being licked by tiny waves, but he couldn't see that. It would be the first to topple. The stones he'd made into a fence around its perimeter were shifting in the small surf. I was about to point out the weaknesses, to tell him to abandon the castle and start again farther in, but I couldn't break it to him. He'd put his heart into that castle, and I wanted it to work as badly as he did. I grabbed a broken bulrush that had floated in and stood up, pointing it into the sky.

"Long live the king!" I cried out. Wasn't that what the Brits said, when their monarch died?

"Long live the king!" Sammy shouted, stretching his short arms out of that orange life jacket as far as they could go.

"Come here." I walked about ten steps to the end of our small beach, out of Donna's view, and Sammy trotted behind me. When he was close enough, I squeezed the two black clips on his life jacket's straps and popped it open.

I kissed his cheek. "Our secret," I whispered.

Viable

In her house, Juna told him, everything had to be homemade. Juna was loading textbooks from her locker into her backpack, math on the bottom, English on top. "How far do you take that?" Stavros asked her. "I mean, beyond bread? Do you grow wheat, like the Little Red Hen?"

Juna laughed. "Let me tell you, we take it as far as it can go in the grimy heart of the city." She paused. "My mother is—well, you'll see."

"She's what?" Stavros touched Juna's earring, the one made from a feather and a rosy glass bead.

"Kind of like that earring," Juna said. "No, like me wearing this earring here, and this one over here." She lifted her hair away from her hidden ear to reveal a gold stud, its shine gone.

"Different," Stavros said.

"Think of other words."

"Unique?"

"Turn that one inside out and you're getting closer."

"I can't wait," he said. How weird could she be, with a daughter as rad as this? "Anything else I should know? Should we bring something, like for lunch? Corn chips, salsa?"

Juna pulled on the hemp cord to cinch her bag. She looked at Stavros and shrugged, her face red. "Toilet paper," she said. "Unless you're comfortable with what we use."

Stavros went cold. There were substitutes for toilet paper?

He'd known Juna for a couple of years, and now she was tutoring him in a few subjects, just to get him up to par after the accident. It was something people liked to talk about, getting body-checked into the boards so hard that two thoracic vertebrae and a collarbone had snapped. He'd had to take a year off, between Grades 11 and 12, to recover. Juna was a year younger, but her brain worked in ways that amazed him. That was what he liked about her; that and her curves, her shy glances between the strands of her bangs.

* * *

After a slow, sweet walk, they arrived at her house. At the door, made of planks of grey driftwood, they could smell garlic frying.

"No vampires here," he said.

Juna smiled. "No, but we do have bats." Then, in a louder voice, she called out, "Mom, we're here!" and opened the door.

Stavros had to duck to get through the entrance, but down in the living area, he could straighten up to his full six feet.

Juna's mother was stirring a mix of veggies in a giant wok. "Hi! I'm Diana. Welcome!" she cried. "Juna, take over here so I can give this boy a proper greeting."

Juna took the spoon and shrugged at Stavros.

Diana opened her arms, closed her eyes, and said, "Give me a hug."

Stavros had never hugged such a short woman. Her head burrowed into his belly, and his hands, when they hugged her, pressed into shoulder blades no bigger than playing cards.

"You smell good," she said, still holding on tight. "Like wood shavings."

Stavros laughed and gently extricated himself from her. "I was, um, sanding something last night in this shirt."

"Oh, really? Juna, is he one of us?"

"I don't know, Mom."

"Are you?" Diana asked Stavros, seductively.

"I'm not sure what you mean."

She swept her hand through the air, gesturing at the whole room. "We built it all, ourselves."

"Whoa," he said. "Juna told me you were—creative—but I had no idea." He looked closer at the half-painted walls, the built-in nooks, the spiral made of coloured stones stuck right into the plaster.

Diana beamed. "Well, it was a work of love. And it was either this or the rubber room, son." She tapped her head. "Therapeutic, living like this."

"Stir-fry looks done," Juna said.

"Perfect," Diana said. "I'll get the chopsticks!" She turned back to Stavros. "What were you sanding, son?"

He looked at Juna. "Um, a hockey stick?" He wondered if he should have said a desk, or a sailboat. But Diana most likely knew about his accident. There was no use hiding his passion for the game.

Juna pulled out a chair for Stavros. "Here," she said. "Head of the table."

The chairs were made of bent branches, and Stavros was afraid he might fall like Goldilocks when he sat down.

"It looks great." Juna spooned the stir-fry into three big, mis-shapen pottery bowls. He peered into the bowl he'd been given. "Are those, like, beets?"

"Yes, sir," Diana said. "Good for the blood. Women need to eat beets, you know. We lose iron every month."

"Mom," said Juna.

"Would you like some bread?" Diana passed the basket of dark grainy bread to Stavros, who took a chunk and buttered it.

"So how's Grade 12 going?" she asked him. "Now that you're a couple of months into it."

"It's good enough. Juna's a big help with science."

"She's a bright and shining star, you know."

"Mom," Juna said again.

"Well, it's true. And what do you think of your lunch?"

Stavros's mouth was burning. He'd worked his way around the bitter green stuff and chosen things he recognized—carrots and celery—although none of it seemed cooked right through. "Spicy," he said. "Delicious."

"Hot peppers are also good for the blood. And so are the collard greens, and—"

"Okay, Mom."

Diana smiled and kept eating. For a few minutes, no one spoke. To Stavros it was nice, in a completely surreal way. At home no one talked at mealtimes, on the rare occasion they were eating together, but it wasn't calm like this. Stavros remembered having better meals with his own mother at the table. She'd passed away last year.

Finally, Diana said, "So. You know why Juna has brought you here."

Stavros looked at Juna, then back at Diana. "Uh, for lunch? To meet you?"

"Yes, of course," Diana said. "But we also wanted to ask you for a favour."

"Me?" Stavros wiped his forehead with his cloth napkin. He wasn't used to heat in his food.

"Mom, why don't you just let the guy finish his lunch," Juna said.

"It's okay," he said. "I'm full." He wasn't, but the food was too much. Eating was not supposed to be painful.

"We're looking for a . . . donation," Diana said.

Shit, Stavros thought. They know about the family business. They think I'm rolling in it. "Okay," he said slowly. "I'll have to ask my dad, but how much did you have in mind?"

Diana laughed. "We don't want money, honey." She took a deep breath through her tiny mouth—she was like an elf, really, delicate features and bright eyes—and her face was surprisingly smooth for a mother, like maybe all these spicy vegetables had worked on her to keep the aging process at bay. Then Stavros looked at Juna— wowzers. Now there was fresh. "We want your seeds."

Stavros blinked. "I'm sorry?"

"We, well, *me*, more than Juna. We want to get pregnant. I mean, *I* want to." She paused. "I'm still fertile, you know. Forty-nine, and still as regular as the national time signal. So I'm taking it as a sign. An opportunity. I'm just missing one thing."

Juna sniffed a laugh. "A rather important one."

"You don't have to decide this instant," Diana said. "It's a lot to digest."

Stavros looked at his bowl of food, still half full of blood-building ingredients. He felt like he'd swallowed a cement block. They were already trying to medicate him, to bring him up to speed.

Juna got up and started clearing the table.

"What would you like for dessert, honey?" Diana asked him. "We've got yogurt and stewed rhubarb, or some raspberry sorbet that Juna made."

Stavros's mouth was still burning. He didn't want to stay for dessert, but he could imagine how good that frozen fruit stuff would feel on his tongue, so that's what he asked for. While Diana was scooping it into bowls, he communicated with Juna silently.

"What the hell?" he mouthed.

"I'm sorry," she mouthed back and shrugged.

He shook his head. What would he tell them? He didn't want to think about the logistics, but he couldn't help it. Diana's little breasts swung free in her loose dress.

"Here we are," Diana announced. "Sweets for the sweet." She set sorbet in front of Juna and Stavros, and dug into a bowl of plain yogurt. Stavros couldn't stop himself from watching her.

"Calcium," she said, pointing with her spoon at her bowl.

Stavros focused on his dessert instead. It did feel good in his mouth. "You made this?" he asked Juna.

She nodded. "Even picked the berries myself."

"It's really awesome."

"Thanks."

An awkward silence at the table, the scrape of spoons on pottery.

"So what are you two working on, in science?" Diana asked.

"Cells," Juna said. "Mitosis, chromosomes, that kind of thing."

"Perfect," Diana said.

"Listen, I better get going," Stavros said. "My dad, um, wants me to help with this thing, and, I should probably, like, go."

"Okay," Diana said mildly. "But do think of our request, darling. It wouldn't be a true donation, of course. We would compensate you, too."

"Compensate?" Stavros raised his brows. He hadn't thought about being paid.

"We could work out all the details, later, if you really were interested."

He wanted to ask her how much they were thinking, but that would mean he was thinking about it, too. *Was* he thinking about it? He looked at Diana's face, perky and suntanned, not thin and yellowed the way his mom's was when she died. Diana looked happy, even though she was maybe a little hyperactive. She had the energy for another kid. But him, a daddy?

"Um, just one thing," he said.

Juna looked up from her sorbet.

"Would I have to, you know, change diapers, and shit?"

Diana laughed. "Honey, you only have to think dirty thoughts and then give us the results in a cup. We'll take care of everything else."

Stavros blushed. "I better go."

A cup. Better than the alternative. Way, way.

✳ ✳ ✳

"Throw me a pen, will you?" Stavros's sister, Alexa, was on the couch, reading a novel. She underlined passages that she either liked or hated. Stavros thought it was lame. He was at the computer desk across the den, looking up sperm banks, pretending it was for science class. He tossed Alexa a pen without looking at her, and it hit her in the head.

"Shit!" she said. "You're a dolt."

She's right, Stavros thought. And how can I be a daddy and a dolt at the same time? But while he was searching insemination, and how long sperm was still good—*viable* was the word they had used—between ejaculation and injection, he was also looking up flights to India. His secret plan was to travel there after graduation, set off with backpack, sandals, and a portable water filter. So far, the flights were around twelve hundred dollars, and then he'd need living expenses for—how long? He hadn't thought that far ahead. He just wanted to get there. The sad fact was that his father would gladly pay for the whole shot if he were going to Greece, the family's homeland, or anywhere else in Europe, or even Australia. But the whole continent of Asia was out of the question. Stavros would have to foot the bill, and leave secretly, too, with only a note on the door to let them know. Asia was why his mother was dead now, or so his father thought. If she hadn't believed her guru-slash-yoga-instructor about healing with breath, she'd have received medical help in time.

How much would Juna and Diana pay him for his donation? And would they still pay if it didn't work?

Alexa started laughing. "They just named the baby in here *Sonnet*," she said. "Who names their kid after a poem?"

He turned around to look at her. "A poet?"

"Humph. There are better names than that."

"Like what?"

"Like about ten thousand other names. Babynames dot com."

He wasn't going to search baby names. But another teeny question surfaced: if he donated, would he get to name it?

The spermatozoa have whip-like tails to propel them forward through the hazardous and challenging environment of the woman's inner anatomy. Their one purpose is to meet a ready egg. Stavros stopped reading, folded his arms on the desk, set his head down, and closed his eyes. His whole body contained these swimming creatures trying to get out. Not that he was horny—anything but. He just felt . . . too alive. Teeming. And with something that someone might want. Someone with a ready egg. He shuddered and tried not to think of Diana, "as regular as the national time signal" Diana. Instead he went through the steps in his head, what he'd have to do if he went through with it. Sexy thoughts. A quick release into a sterile container. A rapid, purposeful bike ride to Juna's house, where she would take the jar from him like it was the fuel for the Olympic torch. Load up the baster with his offering. Pass the torch to her mother. And then—

"Stavros! I'm talking to you!"

"What?" He shifted his head so one ear was more exposed.

"God, you're out of it."

Stavros sat up and looked at Alexa. "I was chillin', okay?"

"Did you get Dad the present?"

"Damn." He'd completely spaced his errand after the bomb Diana and Juna had dropped. Their father's birthday was in two days and he and Alexa were buying him an iPod. "Sorry, Lex. I'll get it first thing tomorrow."

She sighed and got up from the couch. "It's your last chance," she said. "We need to have time to load it."

"I'll do it." He exited the page he'd been looking at seconds before she got close enough to read it.

"Whatcha hiding?" she asked him. "Stealing essays?"

"Just research," he said.

Alexa yawned. "Just wait 'til you're in college, little brother. The fun never ends." She was two years ahead of him, studying to be an accountant. She still lived at home, and led a quiet, boring life. Stavros had thought that she might have gone the other way after their mother died—turned wild with the sadness, and the freedom—but here she was, living like a nun.

"Hey, how tall was Mom?" he asked her.

She stared at him. "Why?"

"Oh, just a project on genes. Dominant traits, you know, eye colour, Punnett squares. I want to know if height kind of evens out, more often, or if kids get one or the other parent's height."

"What do you think? Look at us."

"Yeah, I guess we did get Dad's side of things."

"No shit," Alexa said. "Thanks, Dad." She was nearly six feet tall herself, and always talked about how she hated it. "Mom was only like, five foot two."

"Yeah, that's what I thought."

Diana was at least three inches shorter than that. It would be like pairing a Doberman with a Chihuahua.

"You want to order pizza for dinner?"

Stavros nodded. "Awesome. I'm starving."

"I thought you went out for lunch with Juna."

He laughed. "To Juna's *house*."

"So?"

"You don't want to know."

But he knew that she did. And he could really use someone to talk this thing out with. The trouble was, she would know about the money and then, his plan. Worse than that, she would know about him jerking off, something no sister should have to know. "Let's just say it was a little too organic for me."

* * *

Later that night, after the pizza and a road hockey game with a few buddies—Stavros scored three goals—Juna called.

"Can I come over?" She sounded upset.

"Sure," he said. "I'll leave the back door open. Just come up to my room." Alexa was in her room, watching a rerun of *ER*.

He had time to jump in the shower before she arrived, and was back into a clean pair of shorts when Juna pushed the door of his room open.

"What's up?" he asked. "Besides you." He pulled out his desk chair for her. She didn't sit down.

"This is the night," she said, sounding breathless.

"What do you mean?"

"I mean, my mother just took her temperature, and this is it. The best time for her to meet success."

"Are you serious?" Stavros sat down on his bed. "She asked me today, and tonight's the best?"

Juna nodded. "She thought it was days away, but it seems she miscalculated. Now she's scared because, well, it might mean she's going menopausal soon."

Stavros was confused. "How long do we have?"

"Well, about twelve hours, if we're lucky."

Lucky.

"I know we didn't talk about it today, but we're willing to give you a fair price. And I know money may not be the best motivation for you"—she opened her arms, gesturing toward the whole room, the house, his life—"but it's something, right?"

"How much are we talking?"

"Five thousand dollars."

He lay back on his bed, hands behind his head. Juna came and sat beside him.

"Is that enough?" she asked.

"Enough for me to jizz in a cup? Sure, it's enough." More than enough for India. "But I just want to know something," he said. "If this works out, you know, if Diana gets knocked up, well, what will you tell the kid?"

"The truth, I guess," Juna said, looking down at him. "That we did what we needed to do to make a baby. That's what Mom did for me. She found a guy, and took the rest of it into her own hands."

"Have you met him?"

Juna laughed. "He died just after she got the goods. Bad drugs or something."

She didn't seem too upset by it, but Stavros had more questions. "Will I ever meet this baby? I mean, it's pretty weird, thinking I might have a kid out there."

"You can meet it, sure. But you won't have any responsibilities, after tonight. Or whenever you decide."

They were quiet. Juna lay down beside Stavros and they both stared at the ceiling.

"It's a good price," he said. "For a little of my . . . sap."

Juna laughed. "Sap. That's a good one. We're just going to tap your tree. It won't hurt a bit."

He could feel his cock stirring. "Uh, did you bring a jar?"

She found his hand and squeezed it, hard. "Yes," she whispered. "Thank you."

"I have an idea," he said, and he slowly brought her hand to his waistband. She let him.

"The jar," she said. "Shouldn't we—"

"Get it," he said. "We're on the clock."

He told himself he still wasn't committing to anything, that he could just be lying around with a friend, relaxing. Some of his friends had casual sex with girls on a regular basis, had been given blowjobs behind the school at recess even before they were in high school. He wasn't like his friends. He had an idea about relationships being important, and he wanted one, too, and everyone already thought Juna was his girlfriend, anyway, so this wouldn't do any harm. And Juna was a pretty girl, nice eyes, decent legs, those hips. This was his train of thought, but the train stopped, and Juna's hand kept going, and all that was left was that she did the job quite well, yeah, she was good, she knew how to, oh, yeah, that's it, keep going, you got it, uh-huh, don't, stop, so good, right now, uh, there, there, here, oh, God—

—and when he opened his eyes, there was Juna, her lips red, as if she'd been kissing him, when she hadn't, her eyes wide, shiny, her hands screwing on the lid of the jar.

"Nice one," she said.

Stavros laughed, suddenly embarrassed. He quickly pulled up his shorts and stood up. "Um, how'd you get here?"

"I biked."

"Will you have time to get that home, in time?" He'd learned that viability was short-lived, that it had to stay warm, as if it were still inside him.

"I think so. But I better dash." She wrapped the jar in a T-shirt, then a scarf, then stuffed it inside her backpack.

"Okay, then." Stavros felt like he wasn't breathing. "I guess that's it."

Juna smiled. "Would you mind calling my mother? To give her a heads-up?"

That was the last thing he wanted to do. But five grand for a hand job was a decent rate. He picked up the phone as soon as Juna closed his door.

"Diana?" he said. "It's Stavros. Juna's on her way. She's, uh, got what you need."

She was happy, and started going on about the bad timing, but he told her he had to get off the phone.

Stavros lay back on his bed. Thanks to Juna, he felt relaxed, but he was wide awake and keyed up, too. Would it be weird to date the half-sister of your kid? That idea was like thinking about black holes—it hurt his head. But he liked Juna. The other girls at school were either total OMG fountains or the sisters of death, and he wasn't into either set or sect. He could imagine going on a Ferris wheel with Juna, or on a ferry to an island, hiking in the trees, finding a sheltered spot, spreading out their blanket—

A knock came at his half-open door and Alexa pushed it open the rest of the way. "Juna seemed to be in a hurry," she said.

"Oh yeah, she had to get home."

"You two are spending a lot of time together."

"We're friends. And she's tutoring me, remember?"

"It was awfully quiet in here."

"Lex, will you let it go? Don't you have some show to watch?"

She made a face. "I was just coming to remind you about the iPod."

"I'll get it, okay? It's in my daytimer."

"You have a daytimer?"

The phone was ringing. Stavros foraged around in his covers for it. Alexa waited, staring at him, until he answered it. It was Juna. "It's for me," he told his sister.

She left his room, leaving the door half open. He got up and closed it.

"Sorry about that," he said. "Alexa."

Juna was silent.

"What's up?" he asked.

"She wants me to. You know."

"What?" He didn't know.

"Try it out, too."

"You mean . . ." Stavros couldn't say it.

"Try to get pregnant."

"What, like right now? With the same stuff?" He wondered if that was possible. Or illegal. In either case it felt way messed up.

"In case it doesn't work for her."

"Whoa." He thought of his mother's favourite saying: two birds with one stone. Weren't testicles called stones? Did the sperm he just donated come from one ball, or both? God, the questions!

"What do you think?" Juna asked him.

"You mean you're thinking about it?"

"I don't know."

They were silent for a minute.

"I can see it happening," she said. "It's not that crazy."

Stavros had another vision of them. They were hand in hand in India. They were rafting down the Ganges. Riding elephants. Eating samosas. "Come back over here," he said. "I want to tell you something."

* * *

His mother was supposed to go to India, but then she got sick. An ashram in the mountains, a place to take her further into what she called her practice. Stavros didn't really know what that meant— he knew hockey practices, where you just gave it or didn't, and he always gave it, one hundred percent, because he wanted to kick ass. What was Mom practising for? She was good enough already. Beyond good enough.

If she had gone, would she still be alive? Juna was lucky, even with a wacko for a mother. Maybe he should do it, though, help Diana through Juna, too, in honour of his mother. And his father? Well, if he ever found out, which he never would, Stavros would spin it to make it look like a good thing, another Greek in the world. That just might work.

Maybe he should take something of his mother's to India and leave it there, like they do with ashes. Ashes would've been decent but she was deep and safe in the ground—a privilege to his father because on the island in Greece where he came from, bones are only allowed to stay in the earth for so many years before the family has to come and take them away to make room for the newly dead.

Maybe the yellow scarf she'd always worn over her hair when she cleaned the house. Or a bead necklace. He could break the string, scatter the colours everywhere he went.

* * *

Juna came in as quietly as she had the first time. Stavros's father was in his wing of the house; Alexa's door was shut. It was nearly midnight.

"Did it, um . . . was it okay?" Stavros asked.

Juna sat on the carpet. "I think so. It was still warm when I handed it to her. That's all I did, in case you're wondering. I mean, aside from here."

Stavros laughed through his nose. "Yeah, um, thanks for that."

Juna wasn't smiling. "My mother is just so . . ."

He waited. He could fill in the blanks, but he waited.

"Persuasive," she said.

"Persuasive?" Stavros sat down on the floor beside her. "You mean, you—" Had she taken some for herself already?

"No, I didn't," Juna said. "But it kind of makes sense, if you think about it. Two chances, right, to create a baby? Which is what my mother wants. I mean, it's crazy how much she wants one."

"But if you . . ." Stavros paused. "If you got pregnant, it would be your baby, not hers."

"Oh, no. Not mine. I'm not ready to be a mommy. I'd just give it over to her. It happens more than you know," she said. "A daughter pretending to be sick for a while, mono, maybe, then her mother ends up with a newborn, raising it like it's her own."

He sighed. "It's all pretty messed up, if you ask me. I can't believe this freaking day."

"Listen," Juna said. "If your mother asked you to do one thing for her, to help her fulfill her greatest desire, then wouldn't you do it?"

"Yes," he said right away. But his mother had never asked for more than his love, even as she lay dying in the sunroom. His love, and a promise that he would live a full life, do what he loved to do, and what was right. "She wanted me to go to India," he said. "That's why I asked you to come back over. I wanted to tell you my plan."

"India?" she said. "When?"

"When high school's over. Next fall, I guess."

"Wow," Juna said.

"That's why I said yes to Diana." He looked down at his hands. "The trip money. And now I want to know if you'll come with me."

They were both quiet. Juna picked up a sweatshirt from the floor, shook it out, and then folded it and set it on the dresser. Stavros watched her.

"A year from now," she said.

"Yeah."

"So I could still do it."

"Do what?"

"Have the baby. Look, crunch the numbers. In a year I'd be good to go again." She looked at him through her windblown bangs.

He looked back, and he couldn't help but smile at her perked-up face, her excitement at the new-laid plans. He could feel her intentions in his groin, a ticklish gathering of forces, despite what so many other forces in him were saying. He stared at her lips until they were up too close to see.

After a minute of kissing, Juna pulled back. "Are you sure about this?"

"About what?" Stavros kept his hands on her bum, pulling her in tight against him. "Don't I feel sure?"

"About, you know, baby-making. Jumping into things. I mean, I'm fine with it." She brushed an eyelash from his face. "Make a wish."

He made a vague wish for happiness. He wasn't concentrating on wishes. "Are *you* sure?"

"Totally." Juna giggled. "I've wanted to do this since last year."

"Really? But you didn't really know me back then. I was hardly even around, with the accident and everything."

"I know, but I kept my eyes on you, when you weren't looking." He kissed her again. "I've wanted it, too. More than the help in science."

"So, should we do it again?" Juna asked. "What I did, earlier?" She tugged at his waistband.

"We could," he murmured in her ear. "Or we could do it the old-fashioned way."

"Hmm," she said. "It's way more successful like that. According to all the stats."

His insides started pinwheeling. Success sounded good. But he wasn't thinking about viability. "Okay, then."

As he led her over to the bed, another question crossed his mind. Was he getting paid to do this? He wasn't. That transaction was completed. Wasn't it? This was something completely different. Wasn't it illegal to take money for sex? He wasn't. It was just for a product. His product. Something he could sell again, if he needed to.

Either way, baby or not, he was going to travel, and have a girl— *his* girl—by his side.

"So what do I do?" Juna asked him with fake-innocent puppy eyes that made him want to devour her whole. She lay back on his bed and stretched her arms above her head.

"Just close your eyes," he said as he pulled up her shirt, "and think of India."

India was a nice name, if it was a girl.

Weeping Camperdown

"What makes you happy?" Andrew asked her.

Joni was blowing on her tea and looking smart in a thick orange sweater. She stopped and smiled at him. "Good question," she said. "Do you want a list?"

Andrew flushed with embarrassment. He'd been too forthright and now she thought he was looking for easy ways to bring her happiness, a cheap way in. He smiled at her, but he could tell that his lips looked thin.

Still, she took his smile as an invitation to carry on. God, he hoped she wouldn't say flowers or chocolate.

"Peonies," she said. "They remind me of those fluffy dogs. Shih Tzus, maybe?"

He nodded. A bit off, but yes, he could see it. "What else?"

"My children," she said. "Especially when they're asleep."

They laughed and then the sandwiches arrived and they spread their paper napkins over their laps. She ate her pickle before anything else and the crunch made him jump.

As he was into his first decent bite, she came up with another item for the list. "The moment when you turn off the kitchen lights at the end of a long day. The dishes are done, the fridge is full, everything is put away and ready for the next morning."

Suddenly, he felt close to tears. They were so alike—equals in this ridiculous field they were now playing. Their baggage was of similar heft and vintage. He wasn't thinking Brady Bunch; it was just so good to be sitting with a woman who knew fatigue of this level. The last woman he'd taken to lunch on his flex day had kept talking about Red Bull and e-books and she had updated her location on Facebook right in front of him, as if to tell him that she had people out there looking after her, who knew her coordinates in case the date went bad.

Joni's hand was on his arm now. "And you?" she asked. "What's the biggest happy thing in your life?"

"Ah," he said. "Not a thing."

"Nothing?"

"No. It's not a thing." He'd made a bad play on words and his daughter would cringe if she heard him. At eleven, in her critical phase—another play on words—Maddie was still the joy. "My kid," he said. The comment made Joni smile.

They'd just started talking about their kids when a girl with a pink streak in her hair popped up beside their table. "Are you done yet?" She was about nine, he figured, and more full of nerve than his daughter would ever be. Would he still think of Maddie as his biggest joy if she acted like this girl? He remembered the year she'd made animal sounds when spoken to and he'd had to reassure the teacher that nothing was wrong. Predictably, it had been the year his wife had moved out: another sign of how they'd hurt Maddie. Of course he'd still loved his daughter then, although the chicken noises had made him a little crazy.

"No," Joni said to the girl, who stood there staring at their food. "And we're getting dessert."

Nerve, he thought, was all right when properly used.

The girl moved on, to another table, and got the answer she wanted.

"I don't want dessert," Joni said, after she'd leaned in toward him. "I just want to linger."

Andrew smiled, pointed at his plate. "We haven't even finished half!"

"Kids," she said. "Do you think they're less observant these days?"

"I'm not sure. I'm not that observant when it comes to kids." He didn't like to break things apart, to analyze and compare and pass judgment. He imagined that judging things made most people feel powerful, or more involved in the world. Whenever he turned critical, he just felt old. A curmudgeon was what his daughter called him when he was grumpy.

"Oh, I dunno," she said. "You seem pretty aware." She looked into his eyes and goosebumps rose on his arms. Fifteen again! That's how he felt. He hoped she didn't notice.

"I have an idea," he said, before he even knew he was speaking. She nodded.

"How much time do you have?"

"Pickup's at three, so about an hour?"

"Right. Me too."

"What's your plan?"

"I'm going to get these wrapped up." He pointed at the sandwiches. "We'll eat them, but just not here."

In ten minutes they were at his favourite place in the city: Ross Bay Cemetery. He led her to a tree in the centre of the park-like burial ground and spread out his jacket for her to sit on. There was a small headstone, and a nearly obscured footstone, both engraved with the name MOTT.

"This is incredible," she said, and immediately laid her orange-sweatered self down to look up into the leaves.

"It's a Weeping Camperdown Elm," he told her. "One of only a handful in the whole city."

"Do you visit the others?"

"No," he said. "This is my favourite."

They both lay back and stared into the tree, the leaves arranged like tiles over one another, only growing from one side of the branches. This made them easier to count: a relaxation technique he'd been using since he was little. When his parents started to yell at each other, he used to run out of the house and sit beneath the one decent tree in the backyard—an old broadleaf maple. There he would try and count all the leaves above him to calm himself down.

"I'm expecting gnomes to appear at any moment," she said.

"It's happened once or twice," he told her. "And I hope you like the bagpipe, because they're Scottish gnomes. That's where the tree comes from, originally."

She giggled and turned on her side. "I'm so happy we're doing this."

He heard her words with his blood, his joints, his tendons. Even his bones softened. Soon he was touching her at their command.

When they were done kissing, they both lay on their backs and held hands.

"I was at the library yesterday," she said. "I was just sitting there, reading in the quiet, and it *was* quiet, aside from the old coughing men." She paused, and pointed up at the leaf ceiling. "God! The light!"

It was their ceiling now; before it had been his alone but now he was willing to share. Oh, how ready he was for this.

"Anyway." She squeezed his hand. "All of a sudden, a woman started crying. It was so, so strange."

"Why? I mean, why was she crying?"

"I had to know, too, so I casually got up and moved closer. And there she was, at a table, reading, and weeping, and not even noticing anyone else."

"Wow." He didn't want to think about libraries or sorrow right now—he was under his tree with a warm hand in his and a woman had just kissed his mouth for the first time in three years. The ache of that was so acute, he had to physically restrain his muscles from contracting so he could roll on top of her and—

"Guess what she was reading," she said.

"The newspaper."

"Not too far off."

"Oprah?"

"No," Joni said. "A book on the fate of the planet."

"Whoa," he said, but it was a misplaced whoa, because he'd forgotten, again, that when people said *the planet*, they meant this one, Earth, mother ship. He didn't think of Earth as a planet. Planets were objects swirling with gas and ringed with light and really didn't concern him, day to day. But *this* planet. Well.

"I know," she said. "It made me teary, and guilty, and I got in my old clunker and drove to the ocean, just to make sure it was still there."

"You want to go there now?" The sea was just thirty or so metres from them. He didn't want to move, but he liked to leave his options open.

"No," she said. "I know it's there. I'd rather just stay right here."

She had such a way of saying just what she meant, and wanted, that he remembered why his marriage hadn't worked. His ex had never said what she wanted, directly. She was the queen of passive aggression, and eventually he went mad from the subversive demands.

Joni let go of his hand and turned on her side again. "Do you bring women here often?"

"None 'til you."

She smiled and put her hand on his sternum. "Can I take you to my favourite place, the next time?"

Was she feeling his chest for a jump in his heart rate?

"I'd love that," he said. Then he looked at his watch. "Dammit."

"Already?"

"I know."

She sighed. "Without dust, no rain."

"Okay," he said, slowly, because he had no idea what she meant.

"Raindrops form around dust bits." She'd understood his slow *okay*. "And if we didn't have histories, children, past lives, and so on, we would never have met."

He felt jealous when he thought of her having a husband, even though the relationship was long over. Her honesty didn't help. She'd spoken at lunch about her marriage, described intensity so extreme it made him squirm. Back when they were young, she had pursued her husband in the library stacks, and she always found him. She told Andrew she could find him by his scent, a feral thing. They'd done it in a study room, more than once.

That felt like too much information for a first date. But they were both coming to the table—the grass, the burial ground—with luggage. There were many things Andrew was not proud of, and she didn't need to know any of them, because he had changed. Although he was already sensing that she was the kind of woman who would find out about his past, and he would most likely tell her everything. Men weren't supposed to change, he knew from what his ex had shown him in her magazines, but he was different. He *had* changed. Perhaps he'd become sappy, late to romance, but it had never occurred to him to bring his ex here. Only a small example of what he was now versus then.

"We really better go." She sat up and looked him right in the eye, a challenge in the look. "Promise we'll do this again?"

He rolled over and got up onto his knees, kissed her forehead, then her lips. "I promise."

They came out from under the elm and walked back through the cemetery, under the brocade of branches and turning leaves arching over the path. His hand longed to hold hers but now wasn't the time. There had been no public announcement of anything—no private one, either, but he was lost in the speculations, hope burning in him—so they kept a slight distance from each other as they returned to his car, to the lives they lived, to the world that had vanished while they were lying under his tree.

* * *

Maddie was waiting for him, sitting on the brick fence around the schoolyard, head bent over a book. She was looking up from time to time for him—he watched her for a minute before getting out of the car and walking up the street—but she didn't appear worried. A book is better than a friend, she told him once, and he'd felt both bereft and very pleased, in equal parts. He'd tried to arrange more play dates after that. He could see she had fun with the girls who came over, but she was even happier when they left. Maybe it came down to noise, a lack thereof in her life with him, and she simply preferred the quiet. Their visit to the library was as much a part of his week as her washing her hair, the bottle collecting for the class fundraiser, the takeout pad Thai.

"Hi, honey," he called now, and she looked at him, and then marked her page before putting her book away.

"A bit late," she said.

"You got some reading done, I see."

She hopped down from her perch and walked beside him.

"You weren't worried, I hope."

She shrugged. "You've only forgotten once this month, so I was pretty sure you were coming."

"Good," he said. "I'm sorry."

He'd become good at apologies, and so far, at least, they'd worked on her.

* * *

The phone rang at 9:30 PM, while Maddie was brushing her teeth.

Joni. She needed to see him. He hoped his heart would stay in its cage. Especially when he had to say no, not tonight. He had his daughter.

"I'll come there," she suggested.

Maddie was standing in front of him now, Sears Wish Book in hand. They were going to search through the store catalogue together and circle dreams.

"I'm sorry," he said into the phone, business-like, sorry he had to use that tone. But his kid was watching him, and he didn't want her to know his secret, that he was a man looking for love. This was not a thing he could share with her. At least, not yet. Not until the relationship evolved into something more, if that ever happened, a day when they would all get together and announce the news. "It's not possible tonight."

"Okay," Joni said, lightly, seeming to know he was adopting a voice, an attitude. "But I'd really like to see you soon."

"That sounds fine," Andrew said, more gently. "I'll speak with you tomorrow."

"Work?" Maddie asked when he hung up the phone.

"Yep. Ready for bed?"

"No, ready for shopping!" She held up the catalogue and pulled him into her room, where they lay on her bed and imagined these objects making their lives better. Maddie circled at least one item every two pages, until they got to the lingerie section.

"Eww," she said. "I'm skipping this."

He didn't protest, but he wanted to look, to see what to put on his future list.

* * *

It was eleven by the time he got himself ready for bed. After Maddie went to sleep, he did the dishes, folded laundry, made a grocery list, and answered a few emails. During the weeks she wasn't with him, his evenings were empty; he still had to do the same things but the volume was halved. Fewer clothes, dishes, groceries. He liked fullness. He was not a loner by nature. Nor a single man. He needed a woman and he was not ashamed to admit the fact, at least to himself. The last few years had been hard, but gradually the debris from his marriage had begun to disperse. Maddie was still here, and not debris at all, but the beautiful result of a non-beautiful union.

When Andrew went to the front door to check the lock, he saw that the moon was full. He opened the door and stood on his porch with the light off to get a better view of the sky. He heard someone walking toward him, high heels striking the sidewalk lightly—a woman, alone. He hoped he wouldn't startle her. He stayed completely still, and watched as she came into view. She was tall, and had long hair, and was wearing an orange sweater, like—

It was her!

"Joni!" he called out when she was nearly past his house. "Joni!"

She stopped walking and turned to him. "Andrew?"

"Yes! What are you—what a crazy thing!"

She walked up his short walkway. "I know! Is this your place?"

"Yeppers," he said. "Home sweet home."

"Cute," she said. "I was just out for a walk, and—"

"Come and sit." He wanted to rush over and hug her, but for some reason he was shy.

She sat down beside Andrew on the top step.

"You were out for a walk at this hour?"

"Sure," she said. "I love the quiet."

"You're not afraid?"

She laughed. "Nah." She put her hand on his knee. "What should I be afraid of, strange men on their porches?"

He felt the warmth from her palm penetrating through his pants to his thigh. "It's a pretty safe city, I guess."

"Especially around here."

They sat there looking at the moon. Joni asked, "Is Maddie asleep?"

"She better be. It's nearly midnight."

Joni was quiet for a moment. Then, facing him directly, staring at him the way she had in the cemetery, she asked, "Can I come in?"

He was split in two—one half was already saying yes, of course, let's go and strip down and see what happens—and the other half was holding the reins, as if this whole thing were an antsy horse, a horse he wasn't sure of with all its energy, because he wasn't used to horses. In a second he would have to find out which half was bigger, or stronger, or more in charge. In a second she would need an answer. He looked to the moon for help and all he could see was a breast.

"Come in," he said. "But I'll get you to take off your shoes out here. We don't want to wake the baby." He said this in a put-on voice, hoping she would pick up his tone, for humour. And she did. She took off her heels and exaggerated her tiptoeing as they entered his house, on the way to doing what he had wanted to do all day.

* * *

Andrew would not let her walk home by herself at 1:00 AM, and because of that, she was hinting at staying. He had to say no. "Maddie, she's not used to anyone being here but me."

Joni smiled and stretched her long body out like a slack cat on the rec room couch. "That's good to hear."

Andrew blushed, surprising himself. He was self-conscious about his dry spell, sure, but he shouldn't have reddened in front of the woman who'd just broken it.

"I'll call you a cab," he said. He kissed her forehead on the way to the telephone. She sighed, and got up very slowly, as if she could barely move, like a modern dancer's version of lethargy.

When he had the cab company on the line, he asked her, "Where to?"

"Huh?"

"They need a destination. Your address."

"Oh, right. Uh, 2578 Browning."

He repeated what she'd said into the phone, and then hung up. "You live all the way up there?"

"Yeah, well, it's not the nicest part of town, but it's cheaper than here."

"It's not that," Andrew said. "It's just so far away."

"I told you, I like to walk." She was pulling her orange sweater on over her head. Her breasts, braless still, pushed out from under her Mexican cotton shirt and made him wish, for the tenth time at least, that it was his ex's week with Maddie.

"Let's walk together," he suggested. "On the weekend. Unless you have your daughters?"

"Not 'til Sunday," she said.

"Great." He could already hear the taxi idling at the curb. "I'll call you and we'll make a plan."

Once they were on the porch, after she'd put her heels on and in full view of the cab driver, they kissed. Their first public display.

"Goodnight, Joni," he whispered. "Thank you."

She waved as she walked out to the cab, swaying her hips a little more than he'd remembered. He'd done that to her. Loosened things up. He went to bed, feeling like a hero, already dreaming of the weekend.

* * *

At lunch the next day he told Buddy about her. He kept it basic, but the portrait was rosy. Then, as they were getting their coffees to go, Joni walked past the café.

"Hey!" Andrew said. "That's her!"

Buddy frowned. "It is? That's weird, isn't it? Just like last night?"

Andrew was all smiles as he made a dash for the door, forego-ing the cream. "It's awesome," he said. "See you back at the office."

And it was awesome. Two coincidences like that. Maybe it was a sign, although he didn't lean toward signs. Still, he caught up to her down the block, where she was window-shopping at the bookstore. He wanted to stand behind her and clap his hands to her eyes, like a schoolboy, but he resisted. Instead, he just said, "Well, hello, stranger," and watched her eyes light up, just for him.

* * *

Andrew was late getting back to the office. He'd decided to walk the long way around the block with Joni, who was out looking for a birthday present for her youngest daughter. That was the thing about self-employment he envied: flexibility. She wrote curriculum for online education and her timelines were her own. He had a decent boss, but he still felt the pressure of the clock, and he left Joni at the toy store with a kiss—even more public than last night—and dashed back to his building.

Buddy gave Andrew looks all afternoon, and he deflected them all with blank smiles, busying himself with the Johnson account.

"So that was her," he said when they were getting their last coffee in the staff room.

"Yeah," Andrew said. "She's pretty, hey?"

Buddy nodded. "How long you known her?"

"Uh, well, about a year. When our girls started taking ballet in the same class. But we just, you know, last night—"

"Yeah, you told me." Buddy opened a package of digestive cookies and passed it to Andrew.

"No, thanks. I've gotta watch this now," he said, hands on his little belly.

Buddy took three and set them on top of his mug. "Don't go changin'," he half sang.

"To try and please me," Andrew half sang back. Oh, it had been a wonderful day.

✳ ✳ ✳

When he arrived home, Maddie was already there.

"I thought you had volleyball." Again he'd come upon her with her head in a book, this time on the front porch, right on the step where he and Joni had sat before moving inside. He didn't know if the flush in his neck and cheeks was from the memory or for mixing up Maddie's schedule again.

"My coach was sick, so Jane's mom dropped me off."

"Ah," he said, relieved. "But you could've called me."

Maddie shrugged. "It's okay. I'm really into this book and I wanted to read." She stuck her face back into the pages.

Andrew slowly looked around, at the porch, at the yard. "I have an idea," he said. "Let's hide you a key."

She closed her book. "Really? Like in a secret compartment?"

Andrew smiled, but not beyond what she would tolerate. He had learned the hard way to hide his amusement at her reactions. Often she closed up like an anemone, humiliated. "Something like that," he said. "Help me find a spot?"

They examined every nook and cranny, and eventually decided on the pot that held the rosemary, at the end of the porch. They put the key right in the dirt, in a Ziploc bag Maddie had raced in to get from the kitchen.

"Only for emergencies," he told Maddie. "And times like these. And, it's a secret, so no telling friends. Okay?"

"Okay," she said and gave him a spontaneous hug. Apparently

this new freedom was a big deal. He was ready to give the freedom to her, if she could show she could handle it.

* * *

The next day after school, Maddie went to a friend's to work on a project. But when Andrew got home, his front door was unlocked, and jazz piano was coming at him in waves. Shit, shit, shit. He'd been watched. Invaded. And only a day after he'd hidden the key!

Just before he called the police, he wondered: Would a robber play the radio? Had Maddie's schedule changed again?

"Hello?"

"Hello!" a voice called back.

Joni. She was lying on the couch in a sundress—or was it a nightgown?—reading the book he kept on the coffee table: *The World in Photographs*.

"Welcome home!" she said and closed the book. She opened her arms like she was a showgirl. "Voilà!"

"How did you—"

"Well, I figured you might be the kind of guy who keeps a key hidden, so I just had a little look around."

Andrew perched on the arm of the couch. "That's so weird," he said slowly. "I just put the key out there yesterday." He was still holding his cellphone, 9-1-1 keyed in but not sent. He looked at her, smiling on his blue blanket. "How did you know?"

She laughed. "I didn't, silly. I just wanted to surprise you, and there it was!" She got up on her knees and kissed him. "I thought we could have fun together."

She smelled like oranges. He loved oranges. They reminded him of Christmas and Florida and mornings. He had to ignore the memories right now.

"But, Joni, what if I'd walked in with Maddie? Or what if she came home alone and found you here?"

She sat on her heels and smiled. "I would've hid in a hurry."

"And then what? Slipped out the door when we weren't looking?"

She nodded. "Sure."

"Joni," he said. "We are not on television. It's just—just too weird, coming home, finding you here. Not that I don't like seeing you, but it's just odd, you know? Like yesterday, you just being there on the street when I was out for lunch, and the other night . . ."

He stopped. He felt like he was disintegrating as he spoke, the space between his cells growing, as if he were more empty than full. Porous, like coral. And in those spaces, the truth came flowing through.

She was on his couch, no longer smiling, but fixing her eyes on him with a sort of animal stare, as if she'd been cornered but still felt confident that she could get out alive. Or maybe he was making that part up. Maybe the look on her face meant she'd misjudged him, couldn't believe he'd jump to such a crazy notion, a woman chasing him.

He looked back at her, matched her gaze, and waited for her to speak. He was waiting to hear the words that would make everything go back to normal, a return to where they'd been just a few days ago, eating sandwiches, talking about their children.

She started to cry. And try as he might, he could not just sit there and watch her, waiting for a decent explanation. That explanation did not exist, and never would. He pulled her to his chest.

To stalk was to pursue, to track, to chase and hunt—it meant you were in pursuit of something worth following. There was so much risk these days, with privacy all but gone, cyberstalking, identity theft, and fraud of various types, that Andrew had never given it a second thought. But who really did? Who walked around expecting someone to be hunting them? Who felt worthy enough of this sort of behaviour, except criminals and celebrities? Could this woman, a mother, sobbing against his shirt, really be guilty of this? Did he give off some sort of scent she could track, the same way her husband had? No, Andrew was just an ordinary guy. Not worth any sort of pursuit, least of all with this kind of determination.

"Joni," he said softly. "Tell me what's going on."

She pulled herself back so she could look at him. Her face was red and wet; she tried to smile. "You're not angry?"

He shook his head. "No. Just confused."

"Oh, thank God," she said. "I can handle anything but anger." She moved over to make room for him on the couch, and patted the space. "Sit down, Andy. There's so much to talk about!"

Something in her voice made Andrew's hair prickle. Her expression had changed again, from sorry to enthusiastic. Her eyes were wide, her cheeks flushed.

"I thought we could go here for our first weekend away." She picked up a glossy brochure from the coffee table. "And then we could go back, for our honeymoon, you know, to reminisce. I know the girls would love it—this place even has a waterslide!" She opened the brochure to a photo of the pool. "Isn't it perfect for us?"

Yes, she was definitely wearing a nightie, pale green and covered in tiny leaves. As she spoke, he imagined her buying it with him in mind, because of their picnic under the elm tree. His elm tree.

He began to count.

Her Full Name Was Beatrice

HOW TO PREVENT MADNESS
(too late)

Slide your fingers down your arms. Find the pulses at the wrists, the persistent push of your blood wanting to get somewhere, and fast, to deliver what it's meant to bring: fresh oxygen, nutrients, life force. Imagine doing the same thing to another person, feeling this thrumming, knowing that what lies inside you and what lies inside her is so much more alike than different that you could swap heads and it would be more or less like two universal remote controls. Picture your friend Erica, a woman who smells like pears and wears gold barrettes and has a daughter named Beany who is the same age as your daughter, Angela. Remember the day you took her wrists in your hands to comfort her, over the custody ruling that gave Beany's father more and Erica less. Feel the pulse under your middle fingers before you pull her toward you for a hug, for more consolation. Imagine it being you, your daughter in question, sense the shame in not measuring up in the eyes of the law. Go back to the idea of swapping heads. Do it. Take hers off, put yours on her body. Go home (her home). Watch over her daughter as though she is the most precious girl in the world, as though she's the reason for the battle, as though she deserves only the best from life. See Erica doing the same, only with your daughter, lying beside your husband—yes, dare to imagine even that. Then, swap heads back in the morning. Hug your friend, hug your daughter, agree to meet at the water park that afternoon.

OTHER WAYS IT COULD HAVE GONE

David was awarded custody of his daughter, Beany, in the court battle and that was the end of the story. Safe and sound. Erica, his ex-wife, met a new man. Love all around.

Erica was awarded custody of Beany and that was that. Happy, happy family.

The little girl did herself in. She poured pills into her mouth like they were pop rocks. She exploded into death having fun. La-la-la, look at me with Mama's medicine: I'm a big girl now. But everyone knows to keep medicine away from children. Away from the reach of little hands.

A TYPICAL DAY

A conversation is a beautiful thing, easily dismantled with two pre-schoolers in the room. But the girls are playing with glue and beads and glitter. You and Erica are sitting on your deck, enjoying lunch and the last of the September sun, just outside the open patio doors, within sight of the kids at the dining room table.

Erica asks, "Did Michael want kids?"

You sit back in your chair. "Not at first."

"You convinced him."

"No. He just came home one day and announced that he was ready. I just about fainted. It was like a switch was flipped. Three years of no, and then a yes."

"What changed his mind?"

"He was waiting for the first wrinkle, he said. He looked in the mirror one day and saw a tiny wrinkle, and that was it. He never wanted to be a young dad."

"Weird," Erica says. "As if wrinkles make you a better parent." She finishes her glass of iced tea. "You wanted a kid, though."

"More than a husband." You laugh at this half-truth. You might have gone to desperate measures to have a baby, but it hadn't been necessary. You will never know.

Erica looks up when the shadow of a blue heron passes over the table. "David never wanted kids," she says. "He said he would make a terrible father."

"Are you serious?"

"He thought we were both way too young. I got pregnant only weeks after we moved in together. He wanted me to have an abortion."

"And now he wants her." You shake your head.

"Now that she's toilet-trained." Erica's voice is flat, deflated. "Now that she sleeps through the night."

You pour more iced tea. The wasps are still bad, and despite the jar of honey water on the railing of the deck, there are at least five of them circling the lid of the pitcher. Wasps worry you, but earthquakes are your specialty. You live in an earthquake zone, and every rumble, every quiver, every bass note pulsing through the house from the street makes you nervous.

"We need a screen door," you say. "They're starting to go into the house."

"Beany's never been stung, as far as I know," Erica says. She calls to her. "Any bees in there?"

"No, Mama," comes the little reply.

"They like protein," Erica tells you. "If you put some meat at the edge of the yard, they'll go to it. I've seen wasps carry big hunks of meat away."

You watch as she tears a piece of lunchmeat from a leftover

triangle of sandwich and takes it over to the fencepost.

"Thank you," you say. "But why now? Why does he want sole custody?"

"He's got a wife now. I think she put him up to it."

"A guilt trip?"

"Or maybe she can't have her own."

You roll up a newspaper and kill a wasp on the first swat.

"Watch out," Erica says. "They can smell death. They'll come back for you, mad as hell."

"How do you know so much about insects?"

Erica laughs. "You can take a girl out of the bush, but you can never erase the memory of bugs. Look at this." She points to a round scar on her calf. "That's from a tick bite." You see other scars, too, below her knee, small, healed gashes, but neither of you brings them up.

"Ugh."

You are quiet for a minute. The wasps hum, the girls chatter.

"He won't get her," you tell Erica.

Erica shrugs. "It's out of my hands." Then she studies the tablecloth, unable to look you in the eye. "But I hope to God you're right."

POSSIBLE REASONS FOR DESTRUCTION
(even though many have lived through worse and not gone mad)

See Erica, as a young girl, back in Northern BC, eating porridge for supper and baked potatoes for breakfast because her mother thought it was done that way. This mother had birthed her children with no running water in the house even though it was already the 1970s, a time when all of that should have been over. See Erica, whipped by her father with a chain for forgetting to collect kindling, and Erica, as a baby, set in the oven to stay warm after coming out too soon. See her mother tending to six other children, the father skinning animal hides in a barn.

See a father in the skinning room who wrapped a scarf over Erica's face before touching her, dead animals hanging from the rafters. See a mother who could only, eventually, sit by the wood-stove and die there, hair on fire. See a beautiful young woman who escaped from this hell to Vancouver, where the potatoes were on the plate with the meat at dinnertime and everyone was so clean and quiet. See this woman as she walked the streets where trees touched over her head, reaching out to one another, and watch as she met a man named David who fell in love with her from his men's clothing store window. See how she held his gaze and moved out of the hostel, lived with him, got pregnant, then began to raise a baby. See the baby they called Beany. See her eyes, the same burning eyes as her mommy.

See Erica with the baby. A child-woman, a girl in a woman's life in a girl's body, with a child of her own, on her own. A woman struggling in a one-bedroom apartment, waitressing at a fake Fifties diner, but making it work. A woman who plants basil in her small community allotment garden, despite the cool coastal weather, and leaves space for the calendula, because of its beauty in salads.

SOME THINGS THAT DO NOT SEPARATE YOU

Kingdom, phylum, class, order, family, genus, species
Motherhood, to girls the same age
Gender
Geography
Nationality
A love of organic lemonade, swimming, old dishes, gardens
A fear of loneliness, earthquakes, bees
Language

Access to poison

Access to help

AND SOME OF THE THINGS THAT DIVIDE

Divorce

History of family abuse

Shoe size

Chemicals in the brain

A charge of manslaughter

YOU GET TO KNOW THE ENEMY

You run into David at the swimming pool later that fall. You are there with Angela one dreary Sunday afternoon, and to Angela's delight, Beany is in the kiddie pool, too.

Beany is belly-laughing. She is killing herself as over and over David splashes her and she splashes him back. When she slides down the swirly slide and he catches her, he pretends to get knocked over by the force of her propulsion. She is shrieking with laughter, and soon Angela joins in on the games.

Once the girls are playing games of their own, you and David crouch in the shallow pool to keep warm. You've only spoken once before, one day when you happened to be at Erica's when David came to drop Beany off. Then, you were surprised at David's voice, a deep, booming, confident voice. A voice you could be afraid of, in the right circumstances. Now, you are surprised at his tenderness.

"She really likes your little girl," he says. "She talks about her all the time."

"They get along well," you say, keeping your eyes on the girls, on anything but David, who's moved a bit closer. They're sliding down the little slide on their tummies. The chlorine is making your legs itch, and you're ready to get out.

Then both girls start calling: "Mommy, Daddy, watch this!"

And for a second, as the girls go under and then spring up like roaring monsters, it's as if they are sisters, and David and you are the parents, together. An outsider might assume this.

"She's happy now," David says. "Thank God."

"What do you mean?"

"She woke up screaming early this morning. A nightmare. I didn't know what to do."

You nod. "Angie's done that before. It freaked me out, too."

"This back-and-forth thing is too much for her, I think," David says. "She doesn't have a solid base."

You should say something. Erica is your friend. "Or maybe she has two."

David laughs. "Yeah, maybe."

You look at Beany, pouring water from a pail onto Angela's head, pretending she's watering a plant.

"She has fun with you," you say. "That's obvious."

When David doesn't reply, you look at him. His whole face droops. "I don't want to be just the good-time dad," he says. "But Erica has made anything else impossible. That's why we're going through so much."

"She told me you were interested in custody now."

David laughs again. "*Now?* How about since day one?"

"Really? She said you didn't want kids."

He leans closer. "I love that child more than anything. More than Erica wants to believe. I wanted her from the get-go—she was the one who wasn't sure she even wanted to stay pregnant."

You frown, and lean away. Is he for real? "Erica? No."

"She's a good storyteller. Don't believe it all."

"Did you ask Erica about the nightmares?"

"Not yet," he says. "But I will when I drop Beany off tonight."

"They're normal at this age," you say. "I read about it in a book."

"Yeah, well, the experts don't know everything." He stands up and calls to the girls. "Okay, who wants to go down the big slide?"

Both of them start shrieking, "Me! Me!" and you give David the nod when he asks if Angela can go with him.

You wonder if you should trust this guy, someone you've only met once before, full of stories that you don't want to believe. But Beany is with him. He'll watch both girls carefully. There is a life-guard at the top of the slide, too. People are doing their jobs. The kids will be perfectly safe. You hop into the steam room to warm up while they have their fun, grateful to David for giving you a few moments of quiet.

IMAGINING YOURSELF AS ERICA

Know that you might be making it up, but allow that thought to go out the window, because you are as much of an expert on the subject as the next person. You knew her. You knew how she and Beany lived, and that's what you think of when you create the scene.

Supply list: Blender, stuffies, girl, bathtub, medication, headache, a child's complete trust in her mother.

Feel a pounding headache. Rattle a couple of Tylenol 3s onto your palm, and when you set them on your tongue, taste their smooth, bitter surface before taking a mouthful of water. As you swallow, feel something else enter you like a surge of electricity, like a wave filling a hollowed stone. An idea; a way to deal with things.

Whip your head back to help the pills slide better, and try to relax your throat to ease them down. Your throat is narrow, good at trying to protect you from swallowing something the body doesn't want.

Remember that your daughter has the same kind of throat.

Remember her as a baby, how she had put all kinds of things in her mouth: marbles, a carpet staple, a screw, stickers. Some of these she had swallowed, but not without trouble. The unicorn sticker was the worst, the way it had seemed to cover the opening in her tiny esophagus like a lid. It had made her cries go flat, then wheezy and high. Remember this, how her cries came back to normal when you pried that sticker from her throat. How good you felt when she was finally quiet.

Feel no headache now, but feel instead an idea. The idea is growing into a plan. The plan grows.

Say, "Let's make a smoothie," when the girl putters out in her striped pyjamas. Feel Beany lean against your legs as you fill the blender with bananas and berries, yogurt and maple syrup, everything she loves and more.

Watch as the machine mixes everything together, the same magical disappearing trick you love to watch every morning. It is good to have routines, the experts on split families tell you. Habits, special things to share. Pour the smoothie into Beany's favourite Snow White tumbler.

Notice, when she's finished drinking it, how she is sleepy again. Watch as she lies down on the carpet, tries to get up, and can't. Listen to her crying, saying, "Mama, Mama, I'm sick." See her throw up on her princess carpet, lay her head back onto her stuffed pig, start convulsing again.

Tell her, "It's okay, baby. You're going to be just fine," as Beany's eyes start rolling back in her head.

Look around for something to help you; grab Beany's dog stuffie. Place it over the girl's face, and hold it there. "Doggy will help you."

Do not look away as Beany struggles a little, tries to move her face, to get air, to keep her eyes, wide with terror, on her mother.

Say, "It's okay, my love. Everything is okay now."

Keep the pressure on until Beany stops making any sound, then stops moving altogether.

Sit there, for a few moments, with your daughter's body in the quiet of the late summer morning. Then, quick as it had come, feel the idea leave you. Scream and pick Beany up, run into the bathroom, lay Beany in the tub and run cold water on her, to wake her. Keep screaming. Keep hoping none of this is real.

Run back into the kitchen and find the knife you used on the bananas. Slice into your wrists, but not enough to make you die. Wait for the neighbours to break in, for them to find you, hysterical and bleeding. To find Beany, still in the bathroom, water running over her small, pale face, into her ears and open mouth, into her half-open eyes.

YOU GET A PHONE CALL

Even though you don't like to answer the phone, you always do. It could be Michael. It could be the school. Recently it was a woman telling you to subscribe to *Maclean's* magazine, since it was for people like you. You wondered if she knew you, and how much did she know, and what kind of person are you anyway?

Today, Erica's old boss calls, telling you to write a letter, drop her a line, be a supportive friend.

"She's in the Women's Provincial Detention Centre," she tells you. "I have the address for you."

"What?" you say. "What did you say?"

"She could use our support," she says. "I can't imagine how lonely it must be in there."

You have talked to this woman a few times, and have always thought of her as sane. "I'm sorry," you tell her, holding on to the counter so you won't fall. "I think I better go now."

"Erica tried to kill herself," she says. "She lost her daughter!"

"Lost? Lost? No. She didn't lose her. She wanted to keep her from her father, because he got custody."

The woman doesn't seem to hear you. "She needs us more than ever. It was all a horrible mistake. She didn't know what she was doing."

You could believe in fate, or chicken soup, or the stages of grief if you wanted to. Feeling the sadness. Mourning the one who has died. Acceptance. But these tools are for getting over the death.

You befriended a woman who killed her child, a person who put your own family in psychic danger. What tools exist for that?

"I gave her what I could," you tell her. "I'm done."

But after you hang up, you write a letter. You write ten letters. None of them say what you want them to say. None of them get mailed.

JUST A SMALL PART OF THE AFTERMATH

David is sick now. Pain all over, he tells you, like bugs are burrowing tunnels inside his skin. His life is one big list of should-haves. He visits the gravesite daily and brings her lemonade and Popsicles and cinnamon toothpicks and sticky buns. You saw him once in the grocery store, filling his basket. This is his life now. Beany is gone, but he's still her daddy, still giving her what she loved.

She loved.

You drive past David's house regularly, hoping he'll be outside so you can see his face when he recognizes you. To see how much blame he might give you. How much he keeps for himself.

What you keep thinking: the ripples keep moving out when a stone is thrown, but the stone sinks quickly. Erica is put away, but you and everyone else are still here, out here, without Beany, without the Erica you knew. The one you loved. You still have other friends, but they are wary, a bit cooler now that they know how close you were with a killer.

You haven't made any new connections. You don't know what to look for; you don't know how to judge.

You think of her in her cell, sometimes, when you're lying in bed. You make lists of signs you should have picked up on. Your lists are short. Your nights are long. Instead of sleep, you turn to the mantra of *I'm sorry, Beany*, repeat it under your breath until you must drift off. That's the thing about sleep. It takes you down without you knowing. In your kinder moments, you imagine Erica's madness hitting her like this, something beyond her ability to notice or control.

WHAT YOU HEAR ON THE RADIO

One morning, you catch the middle of a broadcast from a women's penitentiary on the East Coast, after they've completed a survey about conditions. "The beds are hard," the voice says. "The sheets give me a rash. But what can you do? Two years in, I'm getting used to it."

You feel a chill rush over your whole body. It's Erica's voice.

"And how is the staff treating you?" the interviewer asks her.

"One of the guards likes to flirt with me," Erica says, giggling a little. "But I'm not complaining."

The interview moves on, to another woman, who starts in on a tirade about the foul-tasting water. No crimes are mentioned. These women are innocent consumers, complaining about their lot in life. You turn the radio off and sit down on one of the stools surrounding your kitchen island. You want to throw things, you want to weep. You want to call your friend, that one on the radio, because you miss her. Your insides are churning. She still sounds like the woman who sat with you here, on these stools, waiting for the kettle to boil.

Instead you sit like a stone until your daughter comes into the kitchen and wraps you up in her sleepy smell and asks for breakfast.

And what does she want? A smoothie.

One day during her last summer, just days before she died, Beany and Erica had come over for tea. You were outside in the backyard, under the apple tree, seeking its shade. Then Erica went inside to the bathroom. "Wrap us up, Mommy," your daughter said. "Let's play Hot Dog!" You made this game up when she was just a toddler, where you wrapped her in a blanket and then pretended to squirt her with giant bottles of ketchup and mustard, which were really tickles down her sides.

The girls had been playing on an old sleeping bag, so you lay Beany out on the plaid inner layer and rolled her into a wiener. Beany loved it, she was laughing like mad, and Angela helped you to squirt her with the imaginary condiments.

Then you and Angela lay down beside Beany, one on each side, like you were two halves of a bun, and then you reached an arm across and squeezed both girls as tight as you could, without hurting them. You all looked into the tree branches above you, and noticed how many small apples there were, and you made a list of what you'd make in the fall.

Squirrel People

"Who is it?" Sheri was using her honeyed voice.

Dylan should have said the Big Bad Wolf. Instead he admitted his real name and his affiliation—the upstairs neighbour—and after she'd opened the door, wearing a see-through purple negligee with bows and garters beneath, his purpose for knocking.

"Uh, your lights," he said. "Your car lights are on." He pointed at the driveway, in case she couldn't remember where the car was.

"Oh, silly me! I was just getting ready for beddy-bye." She pointed at her ensemble.

"Okay. Well. Have a good night, then."

"Oh," Sheri said, "I will."

Had she just winked at him?

Dylan walked upstairs to the apartment he shared with his wife and daughter and poured himself a vodka and ginger ale. The long day was nearly over. His wife, Jess, and three-year-old daughter, Lulu, were visiting Grandma. Back by ten. He wadded the note and tossed it. He had just enough time for a *Law & Order* rerun.

Dylan had the volume down low because that's what neighbours do, but he could hear them below. Sheri and Mario. He wondered if Sheri took the garters off or not. The thought messed up his ability to follow the crime on the TV show, because that's what brains do—they bring up naughty images. According to Jess, the people below were every kind of wrong. Mario smoked inside,

Sheri smoked more—pot, too—and it rose through the spaces in the old house-turned-apartments, into everyone else's suites. If they weren't screwing, they were fighting. Often they fought outside in the backyard, just below the bedroom window. Sheri swore expertly and spent her days off talking non-stop on her cellphone while tanning and drinking cider from a two-litre bottle. He, Mario, was quiet: he took it all like a scarecrow, a perpetual cigarette at the corner of his mouth.

Dylan could smell smoke now; yes, the after-love puff. He'd never smoked much himself, but he could understand the ritual. He wasn't allowed to forgive them, though. Jess was drafting an email to the landlord, despite Mario's being the landlord's nephew. It's the law, Jess said, and he's breaking it. "And their negative energy is pervasive, messing up your cells," she'd said. "It spreads like an infection."

He didn't feel it; or if he did, he could block it out pretty well.

Jess and Lulu woke him from a nice couch nap, and once he got the whiny child to bed, he and Jess made love, quiet as thieves aside from the springs, then took their creaky walk to the bathroom and ran a bubble bath. Dylan imagined Mario and Sheri lying in bed listening below, mapping out the lives of their upstairs neighbours, talking about them and feeling lucky they didn't have a kid of their own dropping things, yelling, crying out in nightmares.

But the next morning, Dylan and Jess were not startled from their lavender sleep by Lulu's bad dreams. No, they awoke to the neighbours out in the yard, calling the squirrels.

"Hey, Blackie," Sheri said. "Hey, Grey!"

"Watch this." They heard Mario clicking his tongue, as though he was calling a hunting dog.

"Far out, babe." Sheri's voice. "Blackie, Daddy's got some nuts for you. Come get Daddy's nuts."

"God!" Jess sat up, reached across Dylan, and struggled to pull the old window closed.

"Come get Daddy's nuts," Dylan said, reaching for Jess's ass.

She pushed him away and shouted curses into her pillow. She lifted her head. "We've got to get out of here."

He sighed. She was right. It was nearly time for their annual move. He could put it down to bad luck those first two years—faulty roof, no insulation—but this was the fourth year and it was beginning to feel like a sign: this city didn't want them. Jess dreamt of a little cabin in the woods, dipping candles, gathering mushrooms, homeschooling Lulu. But hospitals were not located near the kind of forest she wanted to live in. His work as an X-ray technician was not the portable kind.

"I'll get the paper today," he said. "There should be plenty of listings now that the students are gone."

"Yeah, basement suites with five-foot ceilings and mould."

Mario and Sheri were clapping and cheering outside.

"Blackie ate his nuts," Dylan said, hoping for a little smile. He didn't get one.

* * *

The next evening, the neighbours were at it again: anger as pastime. She was yelling, he was silent, heavy objects victimized as they hit the walls. Then, the following morning, all was calm again in the yard as Mario clicked his tongue and the little vermin came boldly to him. Fortunately, Jess had closed the window at some point in the night, so the feeding rituals didn't waken them. What woke them was Lulu falling off the chair she'd climbed on to reach the cereal bowls. She was fine—just a scare—but while Jess took a shower, the scene in the yard seemed to turn not fine at all.

"You hurt him!" Sheri shrieked. "You fucking hurt Blackie, you idiot!"

Dylan looked out the kitchen window and saw a squirrel, run-crawling away from the fence, as if it had been thrown there, leaving a vague brownish-red spot on the grey wood.

"What's out there, Daddy?" Lulu asked.

"They are," Dylan muttered. "Just eat your corn flakes, sweetie."

"I might be blind," Mario yelled. "That thing gouged my face, in case you can't see me."

"That thing," she said, "is a living creature, smaller than you. And you hurt it! You hurt Blackie bad!"

"Sheri," he said. "Don't get near it. You don't know what it'll do now."

"It's in pain, dickwad!" Sheri screamed. "I can't fucking believe you!"

"What are they talking about, Daddy?" Lulu asked.

"Let's get you some juice," Dylan said. "They're just being silly."

That was their agreed-upon way of diverting Lulu from any harsh reality. It *was* silly—it was completely ridiculous—but he had a vague notion to call an ambulance, just in case Mario really was hurt. But then Jess came out of the bathroom, and he decided to leave it alone.

* * *

The paper had turned up few housing options, so they made the coffee-shop rounds. A kid—even one as delightful as Lulu—was not everyone's optimal tenant, so after breakfast they went to family-friendly places that might have posters tacked up on their bulletin boards.

They managed to see three apartments. All were dismal. That night, over frozen pizza, while Lulu watched *Sesame Street* at louder than normal volume, which felt sadly good to Dylan—a stab at conventionality—they discussed their options.

"We shouldn't have to suffer."

"No."

"We're not the bad guys."

"No."

"We've got a child!"

"Yes."

"It's totally not fair."

"I know, honey, I know."

"I'm sending that email." Jess paused. "Or wait. A better idea. I'm going to get a petition going. I'll canvass the other suites and get signatures. Won't the landlord have to do something then?"

"Don't forget he's the nephew."

"Dylan, you're not helping."

"You're right," he said, even though he had helped, having carried his daughter the twelve blocks home. "I'll start the dishes."

"Yeah, there are so many." She pointed to the pizza boxes, their three plates. Then she was off to create a declaration. *We the people . . .*

After he filled the sink with hot soapy water and the plates, he zoned out on the couch with Lulu, tripping down memory lane as Mr. Hooper and Bob and Marie talked about not being able to see Snuffleupagus. It made him feel good, that he could still see that giant furry mammoth, despite being all grown up.

* * *

The next morning, when Dylan left for work, Mario was watering the yard, pissing stance, smoke in the mouth.

"Morning," Dylan said and then got a good look at Mario's face. "Oh. Wow. You okay?"

One eye was swollen shut, and Mario had bandages on both cheeks; part of one eyebrow was gone.

"Yeah," he said. "You probably heard."

"Well, we . . ."

"She's left me." Mario turned off the hose and looked at Dylan directly, for the first time. "She said I was too selfish for her."

"Oh," Dylan said. "I'm sorry."

"Look at my face, man!"

Dylan looked. "That's pretty beat up, buddy. Hey, I better—"

"I'm fucked, man," Mario said and tossed his butt into the rhododendrons beside the stairs. "Sheri's my life. You know what she gave me for my birthday?"

Dylan shook his head.

"Fucking boudoir photos. Of herself."

"Wow," Dylan said.

"I know. The best gift anyone's ever given me. And now . . ." He opened his hand quickly, like a magician. "Poof. Gonzo."

Dylan had been walking slowly toward the street, stepping lightly on the wet grass. "That sucks, Mario."

Mario lit a fresh cigarette. He took it out of his mouth and looked at it. "She's even got me smoking her brand."

Dylan chuckled. "Sorry, man. Hey, talk to you later."

Mario sat down on the soaking lawn. "Sure," he said, but he was off on another planet, staring into space.

* * *

That evening, things got worse. While Dylan played dollies with Lulu in the living room, Jess was in the bedroom folding laundry, sniffling every thirty seconds because she was coming down with a cold. She came out, gave Dylan a weird, silent, sideways nod, and waited until he caught the drift to follow her into the bedroom. He smiled, hooked Lulu back up to Big Bird babysitting, and stole away, his mind going south.

"Look," Jess whispered.

Mario was outside, shirtless, in boxers, backyarding with his friends again, talking to them in an extra-chipper voice. "Come try this, Grey! Yum. Come and get it." He was crouching down, staring at a greyish-brown squirrel, and between him and the squirrel were half a dozen cigarettes, stuck into what looked like marshmallows. The cigarettes were lit. "Come on, little guy. Come and try it."

"What the hell?" Dylan said.

"You have to stop him," Jess said.

He sighed. "I'll try."

Outside, he approached the scene cautiously. "Hey, man."

"Oh, hey. Good timing. I'm trying a little experiment. Want to see if animals can smoke. I saw a baby smoking on YouTube, from somewhere in Asia, so I figured it might be possible."

"Well," Dylan said. "But—"

"See, if they eat the marshmallow, from the bottom to the top, then their mouths will naturally end up on the end of a butt. Poof! They breathe in once, they're smoking." He took a drag from his cigarette and blew rings. "The baby did that choice trick, too, you know. Maybe I'll teach these guys, down the road. You don't want to overdo it on the first day of school."

The guy had gone manic. "Mario," Dylan said. "You sure this is safe?"

Mario was concentrating on sticking another cigarette into a Jet-Puffed. Dylan started to uncoil the backyard's garden hose from its holder on the wall and walked back to stand beside Mario.

"Just in case," he said.

"They're aquaphobic," Mario told him.

"It's for the cigarettes. Just in case."

Mario picked up the nozzle and aimed it at Dylan. "You think I'm crazy."

Dylan shook his head. Suddenly he was sweating, heart dancing, as if something worse than water would come out of that hose. "No, no, man. I'm just a bit of a . . . a worrier. Around fire, you know?"

"Sheri thinks I'm crazy. She's got a lawyer now, and she wants half of everything." He looked at Dylan. "I cut the couch in half this morning. I started on the bed, too, but the axe head came off the handle."

The hose was still aimed at Dylan, but Dylan was edging toward the corner of the house, where he could turn and make a run for it. Two grey squirrels were cavorting around the marshmallows.

Mario looked at the squirrels and then at Dylan. "Hey," he said. "I just got me a big idea." He looked at the nozzle in his hand as if he'd never seen it, then put it down. "I'm gonna trap one for Sheri. You wanna help?"

Dylan took a deep breath and glanced up at his own bedroom window. Jess was up there, watching the showdown. "I should probably go."

"Just take a sec," Mario said. "You got a clothes basket in that pad of yours?"

"Sure," he said. As if he could get it past Jess.

He and Jess had met when both of them still possessed a certain quality—courage, maybe, a level of risk-taking—that was gone. Since Lulu had come along, or even before that, even while she was still a thought, a star-wish, a penny-throw dream, Jess had become a woman with more to lose. Sometimes Dylan saw a figurative basketful of eggs on her head, a thing she was balancing as she navigated through her days. And nights. Even at night, she'd stopped initiating anything. No surprise nakedness met him beneath the covers. Her mouth guard was in automatically every night at ten, the sound of its custom-shaped plastic clicking into place a reminder to Dylan that she was more intimate with it than him. He felt big, and sloppy, and needy. A thing to be endured, even if she still said she loved him every night. A person can do anything regularly, once it's in the habit list.

Back before Lulu, they just put up with more—if she hadn't come along, they'd still be in that first apartment, making do with the tiny hot water tank, showering together, leaving the dishes until it ran hot again. They'd both still have full-time jobs, too, and be socking away a few bucks for a holiday where nude time was a priority, or else they'd be long gone from this city, with its condos as expensive as Italian villas.

All of this came to Dylan as he received Jess's look from the window, Lulu in her arms. He should move away from Mario, get back to his wife and child, and leave the crazy guy to burn whatever was in his path.

But he'd caught a chipmunk once, in a cake carrier. He knew how this trick went down. "There's a box in the bike storeroom," he said. "That'll work. We just need a decent stick and some bait, and string."

Mario grinned. "Right on, man. We're gonna do this thing!"

When Dylan came back with the box and a broken hockey stick, Mario was scooping peanut butter and sunflower seeds onto a plate. Dylan looked up at his window, but Jess was gone.

*** * *

They rigged the trap and waited. When Mario handed Dylan a lit joint, he didn't say no.

"Women like gifts," Mario told Dylan. "I shoulda thought of this days ago."

"Chocolates would be easier. Or flowers." Dylan couldn't remember the last time he'd given Jess anything, other than the rest of his giant muffin from his coffee break at work.

"Nah," Mario said. "Old hat." He dropped his voice to a whisper. "Check it out."

A black squirrel was under the box, licking at the peanut butter.

"Isn't that the one that hurt you?" Dylan asked.

"Yeah, the little fucker. Even better to give him to Sheri, to show I didn't hurt him at all."

"You wanna pull the string?"

"You pull it. I'll give you a signal when he's right underneath. Watch for this." Mario nodded twice, quickly, then got into position.

Dylan's heart started racing, as if he were back in Grade 6, spying on girls, or waiting to trip the bullies. He felt good. Alive.

He watched Mario with the attention of a raptor, waited for the nod, and when it came—BOOM!—the box fell before he'd even realized he'd pulled the string.

"Bingo!" Mario cried and ran over to hold the box down tight against the grass.

"Nice one, Mario." High-five.

"Team effort, man. Like fucking *Sesame Street* here. Co-operation."

Dylan wondered if he'd been listening in on Lulu's TV habits. Of course he had; the floors were like cardboard.

"Just one problem," Mario said. "How do I get this guy to Sheri?"

"I've got just the thing!" Dylan had seen an old cat carrier down the street in a free pile. He raced, found it still there, and sprinted back, feeling like a torchbearer.

Mario was stoked. They got Blackie in the carrier by ripping one end off the box and jamming the opening of the plastic cat kennel in front of it, and once the squirrel made the move, Mario was on his way, grinning like the madman Dylan believed he was.

＊ ＊ ＊

In the apartment, Lulu was already asleep for the night. Jess was on the iPad, scrolling through apartment listings, with Mozart quietly playing in the background.

"Well, we did it," he said.

Jess didn't acknowledge him.

"Jessie," he said. "He's crazy, but he's harmless. I think if we talked to him he'd cut back on the smokes."

Nothing. Scroll, scroll, tap, scroll.

"You find anything?"

Jess sighed. "Mostly one bedrooms."

"Shitty."

"I dunno," she said.

"What do you mean?"

She looked his way. "You stink like pot."

He nodded, inwardly panicking. Was she moving out without him? "I'll take a shower."

"A one bedroom is all we can afford, in the good neighbourhoods."

Ah, good. It was only money again. "I'll get another job," he said. "Whatever it takes. Unless we change our minds and stay here. I like this place. The tub, the light—"

Jess was shaking her head, pointing at the floor. "Not on your life."

* * *

At 7:00 AM, pounding on the door awakened them.

"Dylan! Open up, man!"

Mario was holding the squirrel cage. "He's dead." He thrust the cage toward Dylan. "The little bugger died on us."

It seemed true—Blackie was motionless, laid out on his side.

"Shitty," Dylan said. "I thought you were taking him to Sheri yesterday."

"I couldn't find her."

"Daddy?" Lulu was suddenly hugging his legs. "Have breakfast now?"

"I don't know what to do, man." He set the cage down. "It's like everything I touch turns to effing dust."

He said effing, in front of Lulu. He wasn't such a bad guy.

"Dylan," Jess called, in a thick, smoker's bark. Her cold was worse.

"Hang on," he said to Mario. He swung Lulu up onto his hip and went into the bedroom.

"Get him out of here," she growled. She opened up the covers for Lulu, who snuggled into Dylan's spot.

Nothing. He had nothing to say. He just nodded and went back to his new buddy and his new buddy's new pet, a pet with a serious health problem.

Mario was looking at the photo collage on the wall. He turned to Dylan, wet-eyed. "You're a lucky son of a bitch."

"Thanks, man."

"What's your secret?"

"To what, marriage?"

"Yeah. The domestic life."

Dylan wanted to laugh. It was like asking a priest about his sex life, a jobless man about ways to get hired. He shrugged. "Showing up?"

Mario stared at him, silent for a golden moment. "Exactamundo," he said and thumped him on the shoulder, hard. "Dude. You are a genius." He moved toward the door. "I gotta go, man. Sheri texted me. She's at her mother's now, and she'll have to leave for work soon. I just gotta get down on my knees, you know. Show up. I think she just might take me back! Thanks, eh?"

Lulu came tottering out. She peered into the cage, hunched over like an old woman tending to the fire. "Kitty?" she asked. She smiled at Dylan, a bright smile as though she was looking at a Christmas tree.

The feeling came to Dylan's scalp first: a slow trickle, like the fist-as-egg trick his brother used to do on the top of his head. The tingle spread to his face, then his arms, and soon he had the shivers all over. He knew what he had to do. He had to find the missing piece of this puzzle called his family. Lulu was lovely—a gem of a girl—but she was still lacking a winning edge, or something. Jess was incredibly stressed, to say the least. And he was . . . lonely. The fact of it hit him like he'd been shoved.

He had a dead squirrel at his feet and a kid who couldn't tell the difference between a cat and a rodent. How could he even think of raising a child in such a sterile home? She was shaking the cat carrier and Jess was shouting at him and he knew only that his next step was to go out and get them a pet.

He picked up his daughter and took her back in to Jess. "He's gone," he said. "And I need to go out for a bit."

"I'm sick," Jess said. "My throat is on fire."

He leaned down and kissed her forehead. She had a sick-sweet smell about her. "Stay in bed, and I'll bring home something that will make you feel better."

"A babysitter?"

"I'll take her with me."

"No. Not if it involves that psycho."

"No, no. He's off trying to win Sheri back."

"Oh, great."

"Come on, Lulu, let's go get you ready."

While she was in the bathroom, calling out for him to wipe her bum, Dylan was disposing of the body. He opened the cage door, tipped the carrier until Blackie slid into a wrinkled gift bag, and after folding the edges down and sticking them closed with a piece of tape, he ran outside and deposited the bag into the dumpster.

Lulu was off the toilet when he came back in, running around with no pants, chanting, "I did it! I did it!" She had a piece of toilet paper stuck to her rear.

"Hooray!" he shouted and told her to get her pants back on. He knew he should do a re-wipe but what would that do for her confidence? He was ready for changes. He didn't want to wipe bums any more. Besides, if Lulu smelled a bit off, it would go completely unnoticed at the pound.

* * *

Two hours later, they brought home their salvation: a fur-faced wonder, a beast of cuteness even Lulu couldn't match. Jess was still in bed, so they didn't wake her on purpose. She woke up from all the commotion—the galloping of four paws, the squeals of joy—and found them in the living room. Dylan really felt better than he had in months. Animals were therapeutic. They gave unconditional love, and didn't care what you wore or smelled like. Really, they were models of the ultimate parent.

What followed was not pretty. Snot and tears and venom and whimpering and fur and names filled the apartment. Lulu was put back in front of Oscar the Grouch, while Jess and Dylan took it into the bedroom. The fight—an understatement—was on, despite Jess's sore throat and the adorableness of the new pet. Yes. No. Yes. No. Ping pong.

Dylan was not backing down. He was on a high, this time a natural one, despite this valley in his marriage. He would keep the dog and Lulu was on his side and—

As Jess stomped away from him, he noticed she already had a bit of fur on the back of her pyjamas. It made him happy.

She went into the bathroom and locked the door—a sign she was not approachable. Lulu banged on the door anyway, saying cute things like, "Mommy, Fuzzy wants to hug you," and "Fuzzy's licking my face now and it tickles! Help!" and bursting out in giggles.

Betrayal was what Jess had called it in the bedroom, and it was the word she said again when she emerged, her face a bloated pink-and-white map to somewhere he didn't want to go. He was using Lulu as a tool. How could he put her in this position?

In other words, they couldn't take the animal away from Lulu now. She was already in love.

He had doubted Jess's theories before, about the energy of others affecting them in all those other places they'd lived with shared walls, but he was starting to think there was something to those theories. In fact, just the other day at work, he'd read of a Japanese man doing crazy things with water. He spoke certain words around vessels filled with water, and the molecules changed shape. When he said, *Thank you*, a beautiful crystal formed. When he said, *I hate you*, the shape went wonky and asymmetrical. If water could shift with only a word, why not humans? Some alien on *Star Trek* had called people "ugly bags of mostly water." It was starting to add up.

Jess was turning into a Sheri, raging about something when no raging was necessary. And wasn't he turning into a Mario, just a simple guy out to make people happy?

He would get Jess some lingerie, and flowers, and candy, put a dollar value on his devotion and see what happened. Or maybe she would just come around and lighten up. Because Mario and Sheri were in the backyard, both of them laughing. Dylan closed his eyes and made a wish. Fuzzy came over, and gave him a watery kiss, right on the lips.

ACKNOWLEDGMENTS

First and foremost, this book could not exist without my husband, Ryan Rock. His relentless optimism, faith, dish duty, tennis matches, and love have carried me through. My daughter, Avery Jane, provided, among countless other blessings, beautiful songs, chocolate cream pie, and honest answers to my question, *Does this sound okay?* Your patience, my dears, has been superhuman. Thank you.

Thanks to my parents, Joyce Paul and Jim Paul, for believing in me. To my siblings, Janey, Jessica, and Jon, as well as my dear Nana, Dorothy Paul, and my stepson, Jonah Brown, thank you for being a superlative cheering section.

A big shout-out to my writing cohorts:

Fiction Bitches, current and past: Patricia Young, Arleen Paré, Barbara Henderson, Claudia Haagen, Cynthia Woodman Kerkham, Jill Margo, Dede Crane, and Lisa Baldissera. The WWC: Laurie Elmquist, Kari Jones, and Alisa Gordaneer. My Writamin buddies: Traci Skuce, Jenny Vester, and Sarah Selecky. My Montreal writing pals: Alice Zorn, Kathleen Winter, and Lina Gordaneer. All offered their eyes and ears to early versions of these stories.

Thanks, also, to:

Everyone at Brindle & Glass—Taryn Boyd, Pete Kohut, Cailey Cavallin, Tori Elliott, and Emily Shorthouse.

Holley Rubinsky, my editor extraordinaire, whose keen and incisive editing helped to make these stories better.

Ruth Linka, for believing in this book when it was just a bunch of stories.

Annabel Lyon, for her help on early versions of "Her Full Name Was Beatrice" and "Tropical Dreams."

Dawn and Terry Jones, and Jecka Meertens of Victoria, BC, and

Quentin and Mariana of Izcatepec, Mexico, for their quiet writing spaces.

Audiences and organizers of Planet Earth Poetry, Linden Sofa Salon, and the Pen-in-Hand Reading series in Victoria.

My Twitter and Facebook friends, for their rally cries of support.

Renate Wellman, Michelle Buck, Chandra Crowe, Melina Boucher, Julianne Cameron, Megan Arsenault, and Diana Batts, for their friendship and camaraderie.

The SOMA team, for keeping me grounded in the real world.

The writing community of Victoria, BC, including John Gould and Sara Cassidy. A writer could not ask for a more supportive, inspirational, or encouraging community in which to create.

Readers and lovers of short stories everywhere. Thank you. It is an honour to share these stories with you.

∗ ∗ ∗

Earlier versions of these stories appeared in the following journals:

"Squirrel People." *PRISM International*, 52.4. July 2014.

"Damage." *Little Fiction*. June 2014.

"Her Full Name Was Beatrice." *Event Magazine*. Fall 2013.

"Adios." *carte blanche*. Spring 2013.

"Viable." *Qwerty*. Fall 2012.

"Pilgrim," in its earlier incarnation as "The Pull of the Moon." *The Dalhousie Review*. Spring/Summer 2012.

"Black Forest." *The New Quarterly* (online special addendum). Spring 2010.

I am very grateful to the editors of these publications.

I am thankful for the financial support of the British Columbia Arts Council during the writing of these stories.

JULIE PAUL grew up in Lanark Village, Ontario. She is the author of a previous short fiction collection, *The Jealousy Bone* (Emdash Publishing), and her stories and poems have appeared in literary journals across the country. Her work has been shortlisted for the CBC prize and was featured in *Coming Attractions '07* (Oberon). When she's not writing, she works as a registered massage therapist. She lives in Victoria, BC, with her husband and daughter, and online at juliepaul.ca.